"It was always like that when we were together," Anna said. *"As if nothing else in the world existed."*

Mitch dragged the toe of his boot in the sand and when his swing came to a complete halt, he stood. "But you didn't know what made me tick and I certainly never knew what drove you."

"All these years we've been left to wonder what might have been," she mused as her swing slowed to a stop. "Wondering if great sex would have led to a great relationship if given the chance."

He grabbed her hand and tugged her to her feet. "That's why we should date. By the time it ends there won't be any more unanswered questions."

"How long do you think it will take for us to get sick of each other?"

"I don't know," he said, unable to pull his gaze from her lips. "I guess that's what we're going to find out."

Dear Reader,

Do you ever wonder what it would be like if you ran into an old boyfriend? For me the encounter would probably happen on a day that I looked my worst. One of those days when I decide to just pop over to the grocery store for some milk. One of those days when I tell myself there's no need to dress up. No need to fool with makeup or hair. After all, who am I going to see at such an odd-ball time? I'll tell you who I'll see—people I haven't seen in years. People who look their best making me look even worse. People who will forever have that horrible image of me in their mind's eye.

Life doesn't give too many do-overs. That's what I like about *Your Ranch or Mine*. Mitch and Anna are given the opportunity to see if love they felt for each other all those years earlier is still there. And despite their fears, they put their hearts on the line.

Here's hoping you get that elusive second chance in your own life!

Cindy Kirk

YOUR RANCH OR MINE?

CINDY KIRK

♥ *Silhouette*®

SPECIAL EDITION®

Published by Silhouette Books

America's Publisher of Contemporary Romance

SILHOUETTE BOOKS

ISBN-13: 978-0-373-65468-0

YOUR RANCH OR MINE?

Recycling programs
for this product may
not exist in your area.

Books by Cindy Kirk

Silhouette Special Edition

Romancing the Nanny #1818
Claiming the Rancher's Heart #1962
*Your Ranch or Mine? #1986

*Meet Me in Montana

CINDY KIRK

has loved to read for as long as she can remember. In first grade she received an award for reading one hundred books. Growing up, summers were her favorite time of the year. Nothing beat going to the library, then coming home and curling up in front of the window air-conditioning unit with a good book. Often the novels she read would spur ideas and she'd make up her own story (always with a happy ending). When she'd go to bed at night, instead of counting sheep, she'd make up more stories in her head. Since first selling to Harlequin in 1999, Cindy has been forced to juggle her love of reading with her passion for creating stories of her own...but she doesn't mind. Writing for the Special Edition series is a dream come true. She only hopes you have as much fun reading her books as she has writing them!

Cindy invites you to visit her Web site at www.cindykirk.com.

To my wonderful friend, Susan Powers-Alexander.
We may not be related by blood, but in my heart
I'm proud to call you my sister.
Thank you for all the support and caring.

Chapter One

Thirty-year-old Anna Anderssen never considered herself a coward. Still, she backed out of the café in Sweet River, Montana, as fast as her legs could carry her.

Once outside she pressed her spine against the brick wall, taking in huge gulps of air. Her heart slammed against her ribs and her insides trembled.

Mitchell Donavan. Her first lover. The man she thought she'd never see again...had come home.

She'd been lucky. Although his back had been to her, at any moment he could have turned around. If he had, their eyes would have locked. Anna knew what would have happened then. The surprise in his vivid blue depths would have been replaced by anger. Perhaps even hatred. After all, what kind of woman—

Stop, she told herself, as she had so many times over the past years, *you're not that girl anymore.* But was that true? Could a person really change their character? A frisson of doubt washed over her and it suddenly became hard to breathe. Anna closed her eyes and a mantra—or was it a prayer?—found its way to her lips. "Oh, God. Please. Oh, God—"

"Anna?"

Her lids flew open and Anna blinked against the bright sun. When the person who stood before her came into focus, she nearly groaned aloud. Having a meltdown on Main Street was bad enough. But having one in front of Loretta Barbee, the pastor's wife, was disastrous.

"Are you all right, dear?" Clearly distressed, the woman's hands fluttered in the air as she spoke. The short, quick movements reminded Anna of the wrens that frequented her backyard bird feeder. "You're white as a sheet. Tell me what's wrong. I'm sure I can help."

Help? Anna swallowed a nervous giggle. There was no cure for what ailed her. And, as far as what was wrong, what could she say? That she'd seen Mitch Donavan talking to her brother and had run out of the café faster than a white-tailed jackrabbit?

Yeah, right. Saying that to this concerned soul would be the height of foolishness. Although Mrs. Barbee was a genuinely nice person, she was also one of Sweet River's biggest gossips.

Since a direct answer was clearly out, Anna was forced to try a different tactic. She fanned her face with exaggerated movements of one hand. "I'm fine. Just overheated."

"Perhaps I should get Seth." Mrs. Barbee's gaze darted to the front door of the café as if expecting Anna's brother to instantly appear. "He could take you home."

"No." The word burst like a bullet from Anna's lips.

Mrs. Barbee took a step back and brought a hand to her chest as if she'd felt the impact. But instead of pain, her eyes gleamed with curiosity.

The screen door of The Coffee Pot swung open and Anna jumped. Two cowboys she recognized as acquaintances of Seth's strode out of the café. When they shot a curious glance her way, Anna realized that unless she wanted her reunion with Mitch to occur under Mrs. Barbee's watchful eyes, it was time to get moving. She looped her arm through Mrs. Barbee's and propelled the woman around the corner.

"I'm so happy I ran into you," Anna chattered, before the minister's wife had a chance to speak. "I promised Stacie I'd ask Pastor Barbee if he could mention something in his community announcements this Sunday about the Young Professionals group having their first meeting Tuesday night."

Anna almost ran out of breath before she got it all out. But the string of nonstop words had the desired effect. The suspicious glitter in Mrs. Barbee's eyes dimmed.

"Lloyd should be at the church." A thoughtful look crossed the matron's finely lined face. "I'm headed there now. Would you like to come with me and ask him yourself?"

"What a good suggestion." Even as she spoke, Anna started down the sidewalk. The way she saw it, each step toward the church was one more step away from the café. "I stopped by The Coffee Pot this morning hoping business would be slow so Stacie and I could have a cup of coffee. But when I saw all the customers, I knew she was too busy to talk."

"Once your roommate decided to settle here, she certainly embraced our little community." Mrs. Barbee slanted a sideways glance at Anna. "Buying the café. Resurrecting the Young Professionals group."

"Stacie likes to keep busy." Anna kept her response simple, knowing whatever she said would be analyzed and repeated.

"Yes, well." Mrs. Barbee's lips pursed together. "Hopefully you can convince her to use some of that boundless energy for projects that benefit the Lord, as well."

"I'm sure she will, once the wedding is out of the way." The wedding, or rather the bachelorette party, had been the main reason for Anna's trip to the café this morning.

A smile lifted her lips at the realization that in only four short weeks, Stacie would marry local rancher Josh Collins. When she'd brought her two friends to Sweet River for a brief stay, she'd never expected one of them to fall in love, buy a diner and decide to make this small town in southern Montana her permanent home.

Of course, Anna had never expected to see Mitch, either. Still feeling the shock, Anna let her gaze linger on the active senior next to her, arms churning as she power-walked her way toward the church. Everyone knew this petite dynamo had her finger on the pulse of the small community. Anna experienced an over-whelming urge to ask her what she knew. Why was Mitch back in Sweet River? Was he here to stay? Or just visiting?

Thankfully she came to her senses before the questions made their way past her lips. Satisfying her curiosity wouldn't be worth the price she'd pay for the information. One simple question and by nightfall, it would be all over town that Anna Anderssen had been asking after Mitch Donavan.

So, instead of treading on dangerous ground, Anna kept the conversation light. By the time she concluded her business at the church, she'd had a chance to recover from her shock and plot a course of action.

The next time she saw Mitch Donavan she wouldn't run. She'd walk over and very politely say hello. After all, she wasn't a spineless wuss. She was a mature, confident woman. It was time she started acting like one.

Anna stared at the picture and wondered if Mercury was in retrograde.

When she'd gotten home from her visit with Pastor Barbee, her roommate, Lauren Van Meveren, had been waiting. The psychologist had announced she had a surprise, then asked Anna to meet her on the porch for some lemonade. Anna had barely sat down when Lauren had pressed a photo of Mitch into her hand.

"Meet Mr. Right." Lauren flashed a bright smile. "Survey says…the two of you are perfect for each other."

A distant clap of thunder punctuated the comment. Anna dropped the picture to the table like a hot potato. "Is this a joke?"

Lauren looked up from the lemonade she was pouring and chuckled. "I know. You are so lucky. The guy is superhot."

There wasn't a woman alive who'd argue with that. From the time Mitch had been a small boy in Sweet River, Montana, the black-haired child with brilliant blue eyes had turned female heads. His rugged good looks coupled with a standoffish attitude had certainly caught *her* eye. And with the confidence of a seventeen-year-old beauty queen used to getting her way, Anna had been determined to make him hers. There had been several months of exciting secret trysts before the fun had come to an abrupt end.

Lauren's blond brows pulled together when Anna didn't comment. "Do you know him?"

"I do." Anna kept her voice offhand, but when she picked up the crystal tumbler filled with lemonade, her hand trembled. If Mitch had been any other ex-boyfriend, Lauren would have already known all about him. But Anna had kept secret her long-ago relationship with Mitch. From the community. From her family. From even her closest friends.

Staring into the pale yellow liquid in the glass, Anna marveled at the change a few hours could make. When she'd hopped out of bed this morning, her life had been sunny-side up. Now the yolk had busted.

"Is something wrong with him?" Lauren pressed. "Should I drop him from the study?"

Anna heard the concern in her friend's voice and realized her silence was giving Lauren a skewed picture of her former lover.

"Mitch's family didn't have the best reputation but he's a good guy." A gust of wind off the Crazy Mountains ruffled the napkins on the table but, consumed by her own storm of emotions, Anna barely noticed. "He and Seth were best friends in high school."

Anna let the words hang in the air, knowing the fact that Mitch was Seth's friend would go far to soothe Lauren's concerns.

"I hope you're not hesitating because you think your brother had something to do with the match," Lauren said finally. "I'd never compromise my research data…not even for Seth."

Though Lauren's words were matter-of-fact, Anna could hear the underlying hurt. She leaned across the table and gave her friend's hand a reassuring squeeze. "I know you wouldn't."

Lauren was the most ethical person Anna knew, not only personally but professionally. It was Lauren's research for her dissertation that had brought the three Denver roommates to Montana.

In order to gather the necessary data, Lauren needed immediate access to lots of single males. Anna's hometown fit the bill. From the moment they'd arrived in Sweet River four months ago, the research project had been the talk of the town. Though what Lauren regarded as pure science, the locals saw as plain old matchmaking.

"Even without your participation, I should have an adequate sampling." Lauren's lips curved in satisfaction. "Thanks to Seth."

Anna nodded in agreement. Her brother had "encouraged" every single male within a one-hundred-mile radius to participate in Lauren's survey. That meant he must have asked Mitch. Why else would Mitch do it? The guy could have any woman he wanted....

She stole another glance at his photo. Her heart fluttered in her throat at the thick dark hair and penetrating blue eyes she remembered so well. There was a maturity to his face that hadn't been there at twenty. The fine lines which now fanned the corners of his eyes only added to his masculine appeal. His lips were—

"I can tell you're interested." Lauren's tone turned teasing. "You need to give your brother's friend a chance."

Anna shook her head. "He's not my type."

And even if she was interested, Anna had no doubt she was the last person he'd want to date. She couldn't help but remember the hurtful accusations they'd flung at each other after the town's centennial celebration all those years ago.

"Okay." Lauren shrugged and took a sip of lemonade. "I'll throw you both back into the mix."

"You can put him in but leave me out." Anna could have cheered when her voice came out casual and offhand, just as she'd intended. "Between Stacie's wedding and my work at the law office, I don't have much free time."

The excuse sounded convincing. And it was true. She *was* busy. Several months ago, she'd taken a position helping out local attorney Alexander Darst. The job was supposed to be only part-time, but lately she'd been at the office more than she'd been home.

"We'll be heading back to Colorado soon, anyway," Anna added.

"Don't remind me." Lauren glanced around and for a second her expression turned wistful. "I'm really going to miss this town. And this house."

Anna had to agree. When she'd returned to Sweet River, she'd been unsure of the reception she'd receive. To her surprise, she'd been welcomed back into the fold as if she'd never left. After living in a large, impersonal city for thirteen years, it had been...nice. She found herself invited to christenings, to barn dances and to coffee at the café.

"By the way, how did the estimates come out?" Lauren asked.

The question pulled Anna from her reverie.

"Shocking. Horrible." When Anna had inherited the

home from her grandmother, she'd known it needed some work. But she could barely get the estimate for the new roof past her lips.

Lauren gasped. "No way."

"Way." Anna sighed. "The contractor said the cost is high because the roof is steep and has all those angles."

While it might make shingling more difficult, the peaks and valleys were part of the house's charm. Just like the leaded glass above the large picture window that overlooked the porch. And the high ceilings with the ornate crown molding.

Thunder rumbled overhead and Anna glanced at the sky. The way her day was going it seemed fitting that bright blue had given way to a muddy gray.

"What are you going to do?" Lauren asked, as if Anna had more than one option.

"Have it fixed," Anna said glumly. She couldn't believe the money she'd worked so hard to save for the past five years would now go to pay for shingles, nails and black paper. Her dream of owning a clothing boutique had never seemed further away.

Lauren took another sip of lemonade and absently crumbled the last bit of sugar cookie on her plate. "You could sell. Let the buyer pay for the roof."

"I thought about that." Anna felt guilty even admitting she'd considered the possibility. Parting with the house would be like selling a member of the family.

Every time she opened the closet door beneath the stairs, the lingering scent of mothballs brought memories from her childhood flooding back. The darkened area behind the coats had been her favorite place to hide from her brother. And the bedroom she now used with the antique medallion-and-leaves wallpaper was where she'd slept whenever she spent the night with her grandmother. Though it might sound crazy, sometimes when she was drifting off to sleep, she swore she felt her grandmother's lips brush her cheek.

"Grandma Borghild gave me her home to love." Anna blinked back unexpected tears. "I can't sell it to a stranger."

"I understand this is difficult." Lauren's gaze lingered on Anna's stylish geometric print dress and the chunky bracelets encircling her wrist. "But you're no longer a small-town girl. The place needs constant attention and it's not like you're ever going to live here again. In fact, after you leave, who knows when you'll be back in Sweet River?"

While Anna acknowledged the logic in Lauren's argument, heaviness filled her heart. Her beloved grandmother had passed on. Her parents now lived in Florida. All she had was her brother, her niece…and this house. "You think I should sell."

The words came out in a controlled tone, but inside Anna trembled with pent-up emotion.

"Only when you're ready," Lauren said softly. "Not before."

"Montana is such a beautiful place. I wish I could be content here." Anna glanced at the patch of prairie coneflowers to the left of the porch. They'd been her grandmother's favorite flower. She'd called them "Mexican Hats" because of their sombrero-shaped flower heads and drooping petals. "Sweet River has just never been enough for me."

She saw no need to mention that it had been enough once. But she'd been young back then. Naive. In love with someone she'd ultimately let down.

"You and I are a lot alike," Lauren said. "We know what we want out of life and we're willing to work hard to make our dreams a reality."

Lauren didn't give compliments easily and for Anna, the support was a much-needed confidence booster. The way Lauren talked, the yolk hadn't broken. The world was still hers for the taking.

"Be careful," Anna warned, feeling her spirits rise. "Or I might think you're telling me I can have it all—a new roof, the boutique I've always dreamed of and eventually a family of my own."

"I wouldn't bet against you." Lauren shot her a wink. "A determined woman always finds a way to get what she wants."

Chapter Two

Mitchell Donavan smiled as his golf ball sailed down the fairway of the Big Timber course before veering to the right.

Though his hadn't gone as far or as straight as Alexander Darst's, it had been a respectable hit off the tee. He'd been playing for nearly ten years, ever since he realized that as much business was conducted on the golf course as in the office. If you didn't play, you could be left out of the game.

Mitch had spent enough of his boyhood on the outside looking in. He didn't care to repeat the experience as an adult. He hoisted the strap of his bag over his shoulder and started down the fairway.

When he reached his ball, he paused and stared

into the distance. The vertical peaks and sawtooth ridges of the Crazy Mountains made him feel at home in a way the ramshackle house of his childhood never had....

"When I went off to college, I always planned to come back here," Mitch reminisced. In the years since he'd graduated, Mitch had seen his share of the country. But his heart had remained firmly planted in Montana where the land was beautiful, the people genuine and the pace to his liking. "I just never thought the return trip would take this long."

"What was the holdup?" Alex's gaze remained focused on his ball as it joined Mitch's at the edge of the green.

"Wasn't ready," Mitch said simply, knowing his reluctance had been more complicated than that. "I had to experience the world outside of Yellowstone County before I came back to settle down."

"Settle down?"

The gleam in Alex's eyes made Mitch wish he hadn't spoken so freely.

"I have someone in my office who'd be perfect for you," Alex continued.

Mitch pulled a pitching wedge from his bag and moved to set up his next shot. "What's her name?"

"Anna Anderssen," Alex said.

A roaring filled Mitch's ears and he hit the ball harder than he'd intended. It sailed across the green and landed in the sand trap on the other side.

"Ease back on your follow-through," Alex instructed.

Mitch blinked as if his eyes were exposed to the

blazing sun rather than shaded by tinted glasses. "What did you say?"

"You need to pull back—"

"Not that," Mitch said impatiently. "Before."

"You mean about Anna?" The gleam was back. "Want me to set you up?"

"Nope." Mitch's fingers tightened around the strap of his bag, remembering the blond-haired, blue-eyed charmer who'd once held his heart in the palm of her hand. "I just didn't realize Seth's sister was back in town."

Alex pulled the putter from his bag. "She and a couple friends are living in a big old house on Main."

"Why did she bother coming back?" Mitch muttered as he stepped into the bunker, sand wedge in hand. He forced himself to concentrate and chipped the ball onto the green. He felt a surge of satisfaction as it kept rolling, circled the cup and dropped into the hole.

"Something to do with her friend Lauren." Alex's ball quickly followed Mitch's into the cup. "She's the psychologist who's working on her dissertation research. Didn't Seth make you complete a questionnaire for her?"

"He made me, all right. Went on and on about her." Mitch reached down and snagged the balls from the cup and tossed Alex's to him. "But he didn't say a word about her being Anna's friend."

The name felt odd on his tongue after all these years. Last Mitch knew Anna was living in Denver. And he'd learned that from another high school buddy.

Seth rarely mentioned his sister. Mitch wasn't sure if his reluctance to discuss Anna was because he didn't think Mitch would care, or because he suspected something had happened between them that long-ago summer.

None of it mattered, anyway. Anna was the past and Mitch's eyes were firmly focused on the future. He was no longer the loser from the wrong side of town but a successful architect with his own company. He didn't need to prove himself to Anna Anderssen anymore.

When he ran into her, he'd be polite but distant. He'd learned his lesson. Never again would he be fooled by a pretty face and laughing blue eyes.

Anna paused in the doorway of the Sweet River Civic Center. She glanced down at her dress and wondered if she had time to go home and change. When Alex's last appointment of the day had turned out to be more time intensive than he'd anticipated, he'd asked her to represent him at the first meeting of the area's Young Professionals group.

With the event starting at five-thirty, she had no choice but to come straight from work. In Denver she'd have felt appropriately attired in the stylish burnt-orange sheath she'd worn to work. Especially when coupled with the translucent multicolored bead necklace and designer heels.

But this wasn't Denver or Chicago or New York. This was Sweet River, Montana, where casual attire usually meant clean jeans and a cowboy shirt for men and a skirt and tank top for women.

She scanned the room and felt tension ease from her

shoulders. Though most of the men were wearing jeans, the majority of women had on dresses. Perhaps this wouldn't be so bad after all….

Anna had barely stepped into the cavernous building when she heard her name over the conversational din. Anna turned and widened her eyes at the sight of the dark-haired woman with the stylish bob hurrying toward her, tall and slender with amber-colored eyes that matched her dress. It had been almost thirteen years since Anna had seen her. Yet she'd have known her anywhere.

"I don't know if you remember me—" the woman began.

"Of course I do." Anna wrapped her arms around her and gave her a heartfelt hug. "How could I forget Cassie Els, er, Dodds, volleyball player extraordinaire?"

Cassie had been one of her classmates and captain of the volleyball squad. Though she'd grown up poor, she was smart and ambitious. Not to mention she had a killer serve. No one had been surprised when she'd earned a sports scholarship to the University of Montana. But instead of going off to college, she'd married another classmate, Jack Dodds, and had a baby six months later. The last Anna knew the couple had been living in Omaha with their two boys.

"Those carefree days seem like a lifetime ago." Cassie's smile dimmed slightly. "And it's 'Els' again. Jack and I have been divorced almost five years."

"What happened?"

"Long story." Cassie waved a hand. "One best told over a pitcher of margaritas and a basket of chips."

"You name the time and place and it's a plan," Anna said. "How long are you in town?"

"I'm back for good." Cassie's lips curved up in a smile. "The boys are registered for school and Trenton—he's almost thirteen—has already started football practice."

Anna couldn't believe that Cassie had a boy that old. Of course, if *she'd* had a child right out of high school, that baby would be almost a teenager.

"I told Mitch I wasn't sure if a thirty-one-year-old unemployed seamstress qualified as young or professional, but he assured me I did," Cassie continued. "So here I am."

Anna swallowed hard. "Mitch?"

"Donavan," Cassie said. "He moved back, too."

"With you?" Anna could barely push the words past her suddenly numb lips.

"Goodness no." Cassie laughed. "But I wouldn't mind if he had." Her eyes lit up and she waved a hand at a large group milling around the hors d'oeuvres table. "Mitch. Over here."

Anna stood frozen in place as a tall cowboy broke away from the others and ambled across the concrete floor toward them.

The urge to flee rose up inside Anna, yet this time she didn't move a muscle. Instead she straightened her spine, dug her nails into her palms and waited. *Mature. Confident.* She repeated the words to herself as he drew close.

Anna knew the moment he recognized her because his jaw tightened. Still, to his credit, he kept moving forward. She took advantage of the opportunity to let her gaze linger. His short-sleeved cotton shirt showed off muscular forearms tanned by the sun. Although the majority of the men wore jeans, Mitch had eschewed Wranglers for navy pants. His dark wavy hair, longer than most of the men's in the room, brushed his collar. She couldn't help remembering how it had felt to slide her fingers through the soft strands and—

"You know Mitch, don't you, Anna?" Cassie asked.

Anna fisted her hands tighter and nodded. She took a deep steadying breath and inhaled the tangy scent of his cologne, the same brand he'd worn all those years ago. She'd always loved the way he smelled, the way he tasted….

For a second her composure wavered.

Mature and confident. Fixing a smile firmly on her lips, Anna stuck out her hand. "Nice to see you again, Mitch."

"I heard you were back in town." He hesitated for the briefest of seconds before his hand closed over hers. His palms, once rough and callused, were now smooth and the mere touch of his fingers sent electricity shooting up her arm.

Her breath caught in her throat and she wondered if he'd experienced the same jolt. But his face remained expressionless, his eyes shuttered.

He dropped his hand. An awkward silence descended. Thankfully Stacie's fiancé, Josh Collins, chose that moment to stroll over with a tray of drinks.

"Care for some wine?" Josh asked, his gaze shifting curiously from Anna to Mitch.

"Don't mind if I do." Cassie took a glass of chardonnay and smiled her thanks.

When Josh turned to Anna, she shook her head. With Mitch's presence affecting her so strongly, she needed coherence more than alcohol.

Mitch took a glass of burgundy and grinned. "Looks like someone has put you to work, Collins."

"I don't mind." The handsome rancher shrugged good-naturedly. "This is an important night for Stacie."

"May I have your attention, please?" Stacie's voice rang out over the crowd. Once the room grew silent, the vivacious brunette explained the mixer she'd designed to help everyone get better acquainted.

Anna groaned to herself. When she'd walked in and seen all the small tables with two chairs, she'd immediately thought of speed dating. But instead of racing between potential dates, they'd have five minutes at each table to share information about their business or occupation.

"I love this." Cassie's eyes snapped with excitement. She turned to Mitch and gave his hand a squeeze. "I'm so happy you asked me to come with you."

A twinge of something that felt an awful lot like jealousy stabbed Anna in the heart. The emotion took her by surprise. She'd have sworn on a stack of Bibles that any feelings she'd had for Mitch Donavan had disintegrated years ago.

"It was great seeing you again." Anna focused her entire attention on Cassie. "I'll give you a call."

"I'd like tha—"

"Everyone should be in their seats now," Stacie called out.

"Ooh, I see an empty seat over there." Cassie flashed

Anna a parting smile and hurried to a table where rancher Wes Danker sat.

Anna scanned the room. Only two empty seats remained. Both at the table next to where she and Mitch stood.

Confident. Mature.

"I guess you're stuck with me." Anna slipped into the closest chair and rested her folded hands on the table.

"It appears so." He pulled out the remaining chair and sat down.

Anna inhaled another steadying breath. Then, for good measure, she took one more. She had five whole minutes. More than enough time to apologize.

"Mitch," she began, her confidence faltering as his enigmatic gaze settled on her. "I realize this is awkward, but I want—"

"Explain about your business," Josh instructed, moving from table to table. "Or your job. That's what this time is for."

Anna didn't care about the rules. She'd waited thirteen years to make amends and by God, she was going to seize this opportunity.

"Mitch." She kept her fingers wrapped tightly together, resisting the urge to reach out and touch him. "I—"

"Before I moved back to Sweet River, I had my own architectural firm in Chicago," he said in a tone you'd use with a stranger. Before she could get another word out, he told her about several of his favorite commercial projects before mentioning that he'd recently started designing custom log homes.

She listened to him extol the many facets of an architect's life. As he spoke he kept his gaze focused on a spot over her left shoulder. Despite his cool attitude, she heard the pride in his voice as he described several of his designs. This wasn't just a career for him, but a passion. A passion he'd obviously had since boyhood. Why hadn't she known this was what he'd always wanted to do with his life?

Because you never asked. You were always too busy talking about yourself.

"Time to switch," Stacie announced.

Switch? Anna pulled her brows together. "I didn't get my turn."

"Sorry," Josh said with an easy smile. "You can catch up with Mitch later."

Anna turned back, fully prepared to be a rule-breaker, but Mitch had already risen and moved to the next table. Disappointment rose inside her. Still, Anna consoled herself with the knowledge that once the game of musical chairs was over, she'd have her chance.

But when she finished her last spiel about Alex's law practice and looked around the room, she realized there would be no second chance with Mitch. Not tonight. The handsome man with brilliant blue eyes had disappeared. And he'd taken the former volleyball captain with him.

Chapter Three

For seven days after the Young Professionals meeting, Anna stalked Mitch Donavan. Okay, perhaps *stalked* was too strong a word. But whatever you called it, she made it her business to find out more about him. And the YP meeting was her springboard to all things Mitch.

Whenever she ran into someone who knew him, she'd bring up the YP meeting. She'd start talking about who was there and make sure she mentioned his name.

That's how she found out he was living next door to Pastor Barbee while his log home at the foothills of the Crazy Mountains was being built. It was how she discovered he worked from home. And that he was now coaching the football team of Cassie's thirteen-year-old.

That last bit of information had given her pause. Until she reminded herself that Mitch's personal life was none of her concern. She was merely trying to right a wrong, not hook up with the guy.

Anna flipped open the vanity mirror of her Jeep. Since she'd been small, looking her best had given her comfort and helped still her anxiety. She studied her reflection with a critical eye. From the beauty pageants she'd competed in as a teenager, she'd learned that lips could usually benefit from more color. She pulled a small silver tube from her purse and performed a quick touch-up.

Dropping the lipstick back into the bag, Anna snapped the mirror shut. She'd been parked in the alley behind Mitch's house for almost twenty minutes. She wasn't sure what his plans were today. What she did know was the longer she procrastinated, the more likely it was that her visit would conflict with something on his schedule. Not to mention Alex was expecting her to open the office at eight and it was already ten minutes past seven.

Taking a deep breath, Anna opened the car door and headed up a stepping-stone path to Mitch's house. His temporary home was a small one and a half story built shortly after WWII. The neighborhood surrounding it was filled with similar houses. The plethora of mature trees and flower gardens gave the area a warm, friendly feel.

As Anna climbed the steps of the back deck she could hear sounds of movement coming from the kitchen. While she was relieved Mitch was at home, a knot formed in the pit of her stomach. Would he open his heart enough to see that her remorse was genuine? Or would this trip be in vain?

She'd almost reached the door when a beagle came barreling out of Pastor Barbee's house. The moment the dog saw her, he skidded to a stop. Before she could say "nice doggy," the animal began barking as if this was jolly old England and he'd spotted a fox.

While Anna loved animals, a dog acting as a neighborhood alarm clock was a complication she hadn't envisioned. In fact, she'd parked in the alley specifically to avoid drawing attention to her early-morning visit.

She could only hope that once she got inside, the beagle would stop its incessant yapping. Anna knocked and waited for Mitch to open the door. Five seconds passed. Then ten. She knocked again, harder this time. At twenty seconds the dog put its paws on the step of the deck and began to bay.

Anna dropped her gaze. After only a momentary hesitation, she grabbed the knob. It turned easily in her hand. Her lips lifted in triumph as she pushed it open and stepped inside. The smile wavered when she found herself face-to-face with Mitch Donavan.

Yesterday's five o'clock shadow darkened his cheeks and his hair looked enticingly disheveled. But it was his attire—or lack of—that sent adrenaline spurting through her veins. "Hello, Mitch."

An odd breathlessness crept into her voice, a breathlessness that only intensified when her attention slipped from his bare chest to the well-worn jeans.

It was odd she'd never realized that a pair of jeans could be so sexy.

"It's been a while since I lived in Sweet River," Mitch said.

Anna jerked her attention to his face.

"Last I knew, when a person knocked, they waited for someone to come to the door and invite them inside."

Though "breaking and entering" wasn't her style, if he was trying to make her feel guilty, it wasn't going to work. She could still hear the beagle barking, but thankfully the door muted most of the sound. Anna lifted her chin. "Desperate circumstances call for desperate measures."

He crossed his arms, drawing attention to his muscular chest.

Anna's heart stuttered.

"Desperate?" he asked.

"If I'd waited any longer, Barky Von Beagle would have awakened the entire neighborhood." Anna's heart resumed a normal rhythm. She gestured with one hand toward the back door, but Mitch didn't even glance in that direction. Instead his gaze remained riveted on her.

"Most visitors come to the front door," he said. "Why did you come to the back?"

A simple question. An easy answer. "I didn't want anyone to see me."

Mitch lived next door to Pastor Barbee. He knew how Mrs. Barbee loved to talk. He would understand Anna's desire not to fuel the gossip mill.

But no look of understanding crossed his face. Instead his gaze turned frosty and the temperature in the room plunged twenty degrees. "Why are you here, Anna?"

Considering the way they'd parted, Anna had feared this conversation might be difficult. And from Mitch's tone, it appeared her fears had been well-founded. Still, she was a woman on a mission. She was determined to apologize, to ease the bad blood between them. But for that to happen she had to find a way to erase the tension so he'd stop glowering and listen to her.

Anna made a great show of sniffing the air. "Coffee smells wonderful. Is there enough for me?"

Mitch hesitated for a second then gestured toward the cupboard. "Extra mugs are in there."

When he made no move to get one for her, Anna sauntered in that direction, her heart sinking. Perhaps she shouldn't have come. Maybe some things were better left—

"Cream is in the refrigerator," he added.

The summer they'd been together he'd often teased her about her fondness for cream with a little bit of coffee. Anna's steps faltered and she flushed with pleasure. "You remembered."

His face was a mask, giving nothing away. "What did you want to discuss?"

"Coffee first." With renewed optimism, Anna chose a mug and filled it with coffee. As she slowly added the cream, she cast surreptitious glances at Mitch. She couldn't keep her eyes off him. His bare chest with just a smattering of dark hair was turning out to be a distraction she didn't need. Anna brought the cup to her lips and forced a casual tone. "If you want to get dressed, I can wait."

For a second she thought he might actually do as she'd suggested. Until he glanced at his jeans and hooked a thumb in a belt loop. "I don't understand the problem. You've seen me in a whole lot less."

Anna flinched. In all these years she'd never spoken of their relationship to anyone. Though they were the only two in the room, she felt like putting a finger to her lips and telling him to shush.

"Nobody knows that." A thought suddenly struck her. "You haven't told anyone, have you?"

"I kept my mouth shut," he said. "That was the deal."

The hint of bitterness underscoring the words tore at her heartstrings. Insisting they keep their relationship a secret hadn't been fair. Not to him. Not to her.

"Sit down, Mitch." Anna softened the request with a smile. "Please."

She took a seat first, hoping he would follow her lead. To her surprise he did as she'd asked. Though the kitchen was an adequate size, it suddenly seemed to shrink. And the sight of his bare chest just across the table made her heart flutter.

Don't look, Anna told herself. *Focus elsewhere.*

She dropped her gaze to the golden-brown coffee cake in the center of the table. "That looks good."

"Cassie made it for me," he said.

Anna swallowed hard against the sudden tightness in her throat and forced an equally casual tone. "Are you two seeing each other?"

"She lives down the block," Mitch pointed out. "I see her every day."

He'd deliberately misunderstood her question. But in a way he was right to shut her down. Who he was dating was none of her business.

When a minute passed and she still didn't speak, Mitch cast a pointed glance at a manila folder on the counter. "I have a client coming at eight."

She'd been warned. Just like at the YP meeting, the clock was ticking. Only this time Anna wasn't going to let the opportunity slip away. "Over the years I thought about getting your address from Seth, but I never took that step. When I heard you were back in Sweet River, I knew the time had come."

Puzzlement filled his eyes.

"To apologize." She folded her hands on the table. "Showing up at the street dance with Andrew James when you and I were seeing each other was inexcusable. I'm sorry I did it and I'm sorry I hurt you. I hope you can forgive me."

The flash of pain in Mitch's eyes was gone so quickly Anna wondered if she'd only imagined it.

"You didn't want to be seen with the son of the town drunk," he said in a frank tone, his expression giving nothing away. "Understandable."

He'd made similar comments when they'd been

together, but she'd thought he was just joking around. Now she realized the pain had been real. Embarrassment mixed with a healthy dose of regret. She'd never, ever, been ashamed of him. And she wasn't ashamed now. She just didn't want anyone to discover they'd had a past because that might bring up other questions.

"That wasn't how it was at all," she protested.

"That was a long time ago." Mitch waved a dismissive hand. "Scarcely matters now."

"I liked you. But I wanted what was between us to, well, stay between us." The words came out clunky and awkward and Anna nearly groaned aloud. She'd had thirteen years to plan what to say and this was the best she could come up with? No wonder Mitch looked skeptical.

"Yeah, you liked me so much that instead of going to the centennial celebration with me as you promised, you showed up with the mayor's son," he said.

Even now, remembering the look on Mitch's face when he'd seen her with Andrew filled her with shame. "That was a test."

Mitch slowly lowered his mug to the table. "Test?"

Her heart froze at the deadly calm in the word.

Mitch had never been the kind of guy a girl could wrap around her finger. And while his aloofness had been part of his appeal, it had also been extremely stressful. Anna had desperately wanted to believe he liked her, but he'd kept his feelings close and she'd needed to know for sure.

"I knew you liked making lo—er, having sex with

me," she said. "But I was never sure you really liked *me*."

Looking back, Anna couldn't believe she'd ever thought going to the celebration with Andrew was a good idea. She'd been so young. So foolish.

The muscle in Mitch's jaw jumped. "You decided to make me jealous."

Anna nodded. "If you reacted, I'd know you cared."

Said aloud, the plan sounded even more childish.

"Why didn't you simply ask me how I felt about you?"

She'd thought about doing just that. But to ask had seemed rather pathetic and needy. Besides, there was no guarantee he'd have been honest. "People don't always tell the truth."

Like her mother, who had insisted she'd be proud of her even if she didn't become Miss Montana Teen. Yet when she'd taken second place, her mom had been furious. Then there were her high school "friends" who smiled to her face and talked about her behind her back. And who could forget the boys before Mitch, the ones who said whatever they thought would make her sleep with them. Luckily she'd been smart enough to see through their lies.

Mitch had been different and he'd been her first. He hadn't pushed her to be intimate, hadn't offered up flowery words of love or made promises he never intended to keep. He'd just been himself. And she'd found him irresistible.

"We had to keep our friendship on the down-low

because of my mom." Anna took a deep breath. "I told her I thought you were cute. She told me you were unacceptable."

By the time Anna finished speaking the pain had returned to her heart.

Mitch rubbed a hand across his face. "You never had any intention of going with me to the celebration."

"I wanted to go with you," Anna said gently. "But I wasn't willing to risk my mother's wrath until I was sure of your feelings."

His gaze searched hers but she had nothing to hide. Well, *almost* nothing to hide.

"I liked you, Mitch," she said. "I really did. I feel incredibly bad about what happened. I hope you can find it in your heart to forgive me."

"I appreciate your honesty." The tense set to Mitch's shoulders eased. His eyes met hers and for a second she had the feeling he was seeing her for the first time. "Coming over this morning couldn't have been easy."

Anna brought a finger to her lips and kept her expression serious. "About as easy as eating barbed wire."

The ring of the doorbell interrupted his chuckle. He glanced at the clock on the wall. "Looks like my appointment is early."

"Darn." Anna snapped her fingers. "And we were having so much fun."

For the first time since she'd walked through the door, he smiled. "I'd say the morning was definitely on the upswing."

Anna found her own lips lifting. "True."

"I hate to rush, but I need to answer the door." Mitch pushed back his chair and rose to his feet. "Do you have anything else to tell me?"

Anna hesitated. Coming clean had felt so good that for a second she found herself wanting to tell him *everything*.

But if she told him her deepest, darkest secret, if she told him about the baby, the fragile truce they were building in this tiny kitchen would be shattered. Worse yet, he'd probably hate her. That was something she couldn't bear.

"Like I said, I was young and immature. I made a lot of mistakes. But I'm truly sorry." Anna met his gaze. "And that's the truth."

Chapter Four

Anna went out the back of the house and Mitch headed to the stairs. He'd hoped to take a minute to pull on a shirt but the doorbell was now one steady ring. Instead of making a quick detour to his bedroom, he stopped in the foyer and pulled open the door. Alexander Darst, his eight-o'clock appointment, stood on the porch, a briefcase in one hand, the other hand firmly fixed on the buzzer.

Alex's hand dropped from the bell and his eyes widened at the sight of Mitch.

Ignoring the questioning look, Mitch motioned the attorney inside. In his three-piece suit and Brooks Brothers tie, Alex appeared to be dressed more for a day in court than touring a dusty building. "I'll pull on a shirt and we can talk. Coffee is in the kitchen if you want some."

Mitch had already reached his upstairs bedroom before he remembered Anna's cup on the table. But there was no way to get it now. He only hoped Alex wouldn't notice.

Even if he does, he won't know it was hers.

The thought took Mitch by surprise. As did the realization that he was feeling the need to be as secretive as Anna. He shrugged aside his unease and pulled a long-sleeved cotton shirt over his head. He refused to think about Anna Anderssen. She was the past. The meeting today was about his future.

Of all the buildings in Sweet River, the one known simply as "The Hattan" had always been his favorite. As an architect he could fully appreciate the design of the brick-and-granite neo-Romanesque structure. As a boy it had been the two lizards and salamander on the top spire that had earned his admiration.

The insurance agency that had occupied the building for decades had moved out long ago. Since then family squabbles had kept it boarded up and off the market. When Mitch heard the property was finally for sale, he'd been seized with the idea of owning a piece of Sweet River history.

Although the two-story structure was solidly built, the wiring, plumbing and interior walls needed work. That meant he'd have to dip into his cash reserves to pay for the improvements.

Still, he couldn't get the place out of his mind. He'd

mentioned his interest in the building to Alex—who'd recently started handling his financial affairs—and the attorney had told him there might be grants or tax credits available for such renovations. Mitch had made an appointment to tour the building the next morning.

He slipped the watch on his wrist, grimacing at the time. Anna's unexpected visit had definitely put him behind schedule. Yet he'd hated to see her leave. For some reason it felt as if there was still unfinished business between them.

Shaking off the crazy notion, he hurried down the stairs, boots clattering against the hardwood. He shoved open the kitchen door and found Alex sitting in the chair Anna had vacated less than ten minutes earlier. "Thanks for waiting."

Alex brought a cup of black coffee to his lips. "You're running late this morning."

Mitch shrugged. He prided himself on his punctuality, but he'd also learned that sometimes a guy had no choice but to go with the flow. "I was up past midnight getting these figures together."

"Appears you were looking at figures, all right." Alex glanced pointedly at the cup with the lipstick smudge and chuckled. "Of the female variety."

Mitch ignored the comment. If the attorney was hoping he'd open up, he was going to be disappointed. Even when Mitch *had* a love life, he'd never been one to "kiss and tell." He crossed the room, splashed coffee into a mug, then gathered the folder from the counter and took a seat in the chair opposite Alex. Pushing

Anna's cup and Cassie's coffee cake to one side, Mitch placed the folder on the table and flipped it open. "As you can see—"

"You told me you weren't dating," Alex said at the same time.

Mitch gritted his teeth and counted to five. "I'm not *dating* anyone."

Alex paused for a moment. His eyes narrowed in thought before a look of understanding crossed his face. "So it's just sex."

"No, it's not 'just sex,'" Mitch snapped. A surge of irritation washed over him. If Alex pushed much more, he'd be forced to lie and that was something he didn't want to do ever again.

Lying had been a big part of that long-ago summer with Anna. He'd lied to himself when he'd told his heart it was just a summer fling. He'd lied to her when he'd acted as if he didn't care. He'd lied to his friends every time they'd asked him where he'd been or what he'd been doing. The lies had gotten so bad that shortly before the centennial celebration, Seth had confronted him, asking if he'd gotten messed up with drugs.

But the only high Mitch had experienced that summer was Anna. In less time than it took to get thrown off a bull, she'd become the most important person in the world to him.

That was then, he reminded himself. There was really no reason to cover for her now. Of course, mentioning she'd been in his house when he'd been half-dressed would lead to speculation and more questions.

Questions Mitch wasn't prepared to answer. Certainly not to a man who talked way too much.

"I arranged for us to meet old man Hattan at nine and tour the building." Mitch tapped a pencil against the table. "I assume that still works with your schedule."

It was a comment, not a question. Alex had told him yesterday that he'd blocked out a couple hours in the morning for their meeting.

"Works fine," Alex said. "Anna is opening and manning the office for me."

Mitch now understood why she'd looked so good this morning. Her red dress had hugged her curves in all the right places and the ridiculously high heels had accentuated her shapely calves. Her honey-colored hair had hung loose to her shoulders, the way he'd always liked it. The summer they'd been together she'd often worn it down…just for him. He loved the feel of the silky strands between his fingers, against his cheek….

Mitch bit back a curse. Her unexpected visit had resurrected memories he'd buried long ago. He picked up a sheet of paper filled with figures and shoved it in front of Alex. "Let's get down to business."

One hour and two-pieces-of-coffee-cake-for-Alex later, the men stood on the sidewalk in the heart of downtown Sweet River, gazing at the granite front of the Hattan building. With the large storefront window and a Romanesque arch over the doorway, the exterior was impressive. Though old man Hattan's grandson had stopped by and unlocked the building ten minutes earlier, Mitch and Alex hadn't yet ventured inside.

"The surrounding buildings are all well-maintained." Mitch shoved his hands in his pockets and rocked back on his cowboy boots. He was glad he'd thought to grab a jacket on his way out of the house. Although it was only mid-September, the wind was brisk and the air had taken on a decided chill.

A particularly strong gust sent leaves and dust scattering across the sidewalk. Alex turned up the collar of his overcoat and hunched his shoulders. "It's a nice building."

"Nice?" an indignant female voice interjected. "Look at those carvings. The Hattan isn't just nice. It's the most beautiful building in the whole town."

Mitch spun around. He'd been so focused on admiring the building's facade that he hadn't noticed Cassie's arrival. She stood on the other side of Alex, her dark hair twisted in a halfhearted ponytail. With her well-worn jeans and bulky oversize sweater, she looked like she'd just hopped out of bed and pulled on whatever was on the floor.

He couldn't help but smile, remembering his days in grade school when whatever was on the floor had usually been all there *was* to wear. For him, because his dad drank any extra money away. For her, because her single-parent mom was more interested in her boyfriends than in providing for her daughter.

Though his life had gotten easier, Cassie still struggled. Her sewing ability was the only thing keeping her out of the welfare line. Last night when they'd shared a beer on her porch, he'd mentioned how tired she'd been looking. She'd assured him that with Stacie's wedding dress now finished, she was through burning the midnight oil.

"I thought you promised me you'd sleep in," he chided. The older-brother role was a familiar one for him. After all, he'd looked out for her since they were kids.

"Change in plans," Cassie said with a rueful smile. "Trenton left his math assignment at home."

"Uh, Cassie, the high school is thataway." Mitch gestured with his head.

She shoved her shoulder against him. "I know that, you goof. I was headed back home when I got a craving for one of Stacie's gooey cinnamon rolls. I saw you standing on the sidewalk and wondered if you'd like to join me."

While a cinnamon roll sounded good, business had to come before pleasure.

"Your friend is welcome, too," Cassie said quickly.

Mitch thought for a moment. "Can you wait while we check out the inside?"

Cassie's eyes brightened. "Can I come, too? I promise I'll zip my mouth and be quiet as a mouse."

Mitch had to laugh. She wouldn't last five minutes. "Of course you can come. And talk all you want. You know I value your opinion."

Cassie blushed. "That's nice of you to say."

A look of speculation filled Alex's eyes. He turned toward Cassie and stuck out his hand. "If we're going to break bread together, we should know each other's names. I'm Alex Darst, a new attorney in town."

"Cassie Els. I live just down the street from Mitch." She took his hand. "I've heard so many nice things about you. It's a pleasure to finally put a face with a name."

Mitch pulled his brows together. By the way they were acting, he'd have thought the two were strangers. "Didn't you meet at the Young Professionals meeting?"

Alex shook his head. "I wasn't there. I sent Anna Anderssen to represent the office for me. Remember?"

Of course Mitch remembered the evening. He remembered his shock at seeing Anna after so many years. And he remembered how determined he'd been to keep the conversation strictly business.

"You're Anna's boss?" he heard Cassie say. "She and I are friends."

"Yep. Anna works for me." Alex's proprietary tone set Mitch's teeth on edge. "She's a great employee."

"I don't doubt that," Cassie said. "Even back in high school, Anna was very responsible."

Anna. Anna. Anna. Mitch hadn't heard the name in years. Now it seemed he couldn't go five seconds without being reminded of her.

"Are you and your husband happy you made the decision to move back?" Alex asked, abruptly changing the subject.

"I'm divorced." Cassie lifted her chin. "It's just my two boys and me now. And of course my friends."

To Mitch's surprise, she reached over, slipped her hand around his arm and gave a squeeze.

"Well, if this isn't a motley crew…"

Cassie's hand dropped from his arm and she took a step back.

Perhaps Mitch should have been surprised to hear Anna's voice. But he wasn't. As many times as her name had been mentioned already, it would have seemed odd if she *hadn't* appeared.

"Anna. What are you doing here?" Surprise flashed across Alex's face. "You're supposed to be watching the office."

The hint of censure in the man's voice roused Mitch's protective instinct but he reminded himself this was Anna's battle, not his.

"I *am* watching the office." Anna slipped her hand into her bag and retrieved a hot-pink cell phone. "Electronically. I gave the papers to this morning's client, then forwarded your calls to my cell."

Her smile was engaging but Alex's gaze narrowed. "What about walk-ins?"

"No one seeing an attorney just stops by," Anna said with a dismissive wave. "Since I've worked for you, I've yet to see one person walk through the door without an appointment."

"I still don't understand what was so important that you had to leave the office," Alex said.

"You forgot these." Anna pulled a sheaf of papers from her oversize bag.

The tight lines bracketing Alex's mouth eased. Puzzlement filled his gaze. "What are they?"

"Documents for your ten-fifteen meeting." The papers Anna held flapped in the wind. "I was worried you wouldn't have time to make it back to the office before your next appointment."

Alex took the papers from her outstretched hand and slipped them into his briefcase. A rueful smile tipped his lips. "Thanks. I shouldn't have made assumptions before I had all the facts."

"No worries." Anna shivered and her gaze settled longingly on the building's front door. "Could we step inside for a minute? It's freezing out here."

Mitch resisted the urge to smile. For someone who could be so hot in bed, the entire time he'd known Anna she'd been notoriously cold-blooded. Just like now. Though the temperature had to be at least sixty, tiny goose bumps dotted her arms and nylon-clad legs. Of course, he had to admit the thin fabric of her wraparound dress provided little protection from the wind.

Before he had a chance to think about what he was doing, Mitch whipped off his coat and settled it around her shoulders. He wasn't sure which of them was more surprised.

"I couldn't—" Anna said, even as she pulled the jacket tight around her.

"I'm plenty warm," Mitch said, dismissing her protest. She'd been away from Montana too long. She'd obviously forgotten that in Sweet River, men took care of women. It didn't matter if they had feelings for them or not.

"After we tour the building, we're heading over to The Coffee Pot." Cassie spoke for the first time since Anna had appeared. "Care to join us?"

Anna's gaze settled on Alex and a look of uncertainty filled her eyes. "As long as you don't mind the office being unmanned a little while longer?"

Mitch turned and headed for the building's front door. He didn't bother waiting for Alex's response because it didn't matter to him whether Anna came along or not. She meant nothing to him. Nothing at all.

Chapter Five

Anna stared at Mitch through lowered lashes. It felt strange to be seated across from him in so public a spot. After hiking with him, Alex and Cassie through two dusty floors of The Hattan, they'd headed to The Coffee Pot. The only table open had been the one by the front window.

Three prominent citizens had already stopped by to say hello. Pastor Barbee had been the first, followed by the sheriff. Then Henry Millstead, who'd been Mitch's boss when he'd been in high school, had knocked on the window. Mitch had excused himself and gone outside to talk to the rancher for a few minutes.

Once Mitch came back, Stacie took their order. She returned minutes later with coffee, juice and rolls. Anna could tell her friend wanted to stay and visit but the need to prepare for the lunch rush pulled her away.

"Do you think you'll buy the building?" Anna hadn't even known Mitch was serious about purchasing it until she'd heard him discussing financing options with Alex.

"It would be great if you did." Seated between Anna and Mitch, Cassie reached over and covered his hand with hers. "I'd love to rent some main floor space for a sewing shop."

That Cassie was even considering being a business owner was news to Anna. But she couldn't focus on that now. Not when the dark-haired beauty was holding hands with Mitch. She waited for him to pull his hand away. After all, he knew how people in Sweet River loved to talk. Instead, Anna watched in horror as he flipped his hand over and laced his fingers through hers.

"I didn't realize you were thinking of opening your own business." The warm approval in his voice brought a smile to Cassie's lips.

Anna gripped the edge of the table. She was happy Cassie had an entrepreneurial spirit. Delighted she was considering opening her own business. But Anna had planned since college for her boutique. She'd studied hard. She'd supplemented knowledge gleaned from her college courses with real-world lessons.

She should be the one Mitch was looking at with admiration in his eyes, not Cassie. He should be asking about *her* business plan, because she would understand what he was talking about.

The uncharitable thought jerked Anna from her pity party. Cassie was a friend. She was smart and talented and deserved any happiness that came her way.

If only Mitch would move his hand...

"...Denver?"

With a start, Anna refocused. Alex had asked a question and she had no idea what he'd said. She pulled together her tangled thoughts. "I'm sorry. I missed the first part of the question."

A smile and a knowing look filled Alex's eyes. "I asked if you knew when you'd be returning to Colorado."

"I'd say another three months or so." Anna kept her attention focused on Alex, refusing to glance down to check out the intertwined hands. "By then Lauren will have completed her dissertation research."

"So you plan to hang out until then?" Mitch asked.

Anna swiveled her head. "For your information, I don't just 'hang out.' When I'm not helping Lauren with her research, I'm working for Alex or coordinating repairs to my grandmother's house."

"Whoa," Mitch protested, raising his hands. "I never said you aren't busy."

Anna hid a satisfied smile. Last she knew, it was impossible to hold hands when one set was in the air.

"Grandmother's house?" Alex asked. "Is that the big white one on Main?"

"It's mine now." Anna couldn't keep the pride from her voice.

"I always loved that house." Cassie's tone turned

dreamy. "When I was in middle school, I was drawn to that neighborhood. Especially at Christmastime when I could see the lights on the tree through the lace curtains. I'd walk down the sidewalk and stop in front of your grandmother's home." A swath of red stole across her cheeks. "I used to pretend it was my house."

"You'll have one like that someday," Mitch said.

"Maybe." Cassie shrugged. "For now I'm just grateful to have a roof over my head and food on the table."

"I hate to cut this short," Alex said as he pushed back his chair and stood, "but my next appointment is in fifteen minutes."

"I'll walk out with you." Cassie rose to her feet. "Loretta Barbee is bringing over some clothes to be altered at ten-thirty so I need to head home."

Anna looked down at her barely touched cinnamon roll and fought a surge of disappointment. Although sitting across from Mitch still wasn't entirely comfortable, she was feeling more at ease by the minute. She swallowed a sigh. "I suppose I should be going, too."

"Stay and enjoy your roll," Alex said in an unexpectedly jovial tone. "Talk to Mitch. Use this time to catch up."

After dropping a couple bills on the table, Alex hurried to open the door for Cassie.

Anna lifted the cup to her lips, feeling excited and scared at the same time. Being alone with Mitch in such a public location would be a true test of their ability to put the past behind them.

She took a sip of coffee, forced a light tone and smiled at Mitch. "Fancy meeting you again."

He leaned back in his chair. Mitch looked completely relaxed except, of course, for the fingers holding his cup in a death grip. "It's a small town. We're bound to run into each other."

"At least this isn't awkward," Anna began, tripping over the words. "Not for me, anyway. You?"

"Not at all." Mitch released his hold on the cup and popped a piece of cinnamon roll into his mouth.

"Because we talked," Anna said. "Cleared the air."

He brought the cup to his lips. "We did."

She paused, reviewing everything that had happened from the moment she'd walked through his door until she'd left. "Was it Alex at the door this morning?"

"You mean the one laying on the doorbell?" Mitch's lips quirked upward. "That was him."

"Did he know I'd been there?"

Mitch's smile faded. "Alex knew a woman had been there. He has no idea it was you."

Anna exhaled the breath she'd been holding. "Good."

"Ah, yes, your precious reputation." His tone made it sound like a dirty word. "Couldn't forget about that."

Anna frowned. "You're the one whose reputation I'm concerned about. I don't have to live in this town. At least not for much longer. You do."

"C'mon, Anna," Mitch said. "Even if you can't be honest with me, at least be honest with yourself."

"I don't care."

"Yeah, right."

Her heart picked up speed and a curious tingling filled her body. He'd dared her. Just like Seth had done when she was four and she'd been scared to jump off the high board.

To this day Anna didn't remember climbing the ladder. But she'd never forgotten the thrill she'd felt during the free fall into the pool. "I'll prove *I* don't care."

"More talk—"

He probably planned to say more but Anna had already half risen from her seat, then put her hands on both sides of his face and covered his mouth with hers.

She'd planned for it to be a quick kiss. A brief but succinct answer to his dare. But the moment her lips touched his, she was caught in a web of desire.

Even after all these years, the taste of him was both familiar…and erotic. With her heart hammering against her chest and want coursing through her veins, she opened her mouth—

"What the hell is going on here?"

Anna jerked back. Seth stood next to the table, his eyes flashing blue fire.

She stifled a groan. Big brother to the rescue.

"Do you want to tell me what you're doing?" Seth's voice was as tightly wound as a barbed-wire fence.

"Watch your tone, Seth," Mitch warned.

"It's okay." Anna flashed Mitch a smile before focusing her attention on her brother. "*I* was kissing Mitch."

"*I* saw," Seth said with an impatient swipe of his hand. "Along with everyone else in the café."

Anna glanced around the dining room. Stacie looked like she was trying hard not to laugh. Norm and Al, who never let anything interrupt their game of checkers, were blatantly staring.

"I wanted to do it," Anna said loudly, lifting her chin. "And I might just do it again. Anyone got a problem with that?"

Al and Norm exchanged a glance and chuckled before turning back to the checkerboard. Stacie gave her a double thumbs-up. That left only Seth.

To Anna's surprise, her brother's face relaxed into a smile. "I don't have a problem, little sister. As long as you and my hardheaded buddy know what you're doing, I got no problem at all."

Mitch had been bucked off a bronc once. He'd hit the ground with enough force to drive all the air from his lungs. Yet, even lying there in the dirt, his pulse had continued its slow, steady beat. But here, now, one kiss from Anna and his heart spazzed out.

It was giving his ribs a solid beating when Anna announced she needed to go to the office. Seconds later she sashayed out of the café.

His heart was still reeling when Stacie appeared tableside, coffeepot in hand. She refilled his cup then cast a questioning glance at Seth.

Without a word, Seth dropped into the chair his sister had just vacated and flipped over the cup that had been facedown on the saucer. "The stronger the better."

Leaning back in his seat, Mitch watched the steaming brew enter Seth's cup. Though he could tell Stacie wanted to stay and talk, he didn't suggest she join them.

He wasn't sure what was going on in Seth's head but he was sure his friend had questions. Questions best asked and answered without an audience.

"What was that kiss about?" Seth asked the second Stacie was out of earshot.

Mitch reached for his cup then realized he couldn't sit still another second. He couldn't pretend to be civilized and unaffected. Not when his thoughts were as tangled as tumbleweed and his lips still yearned for the sweet taste of Anna's kiss.

Plunging his hand into a pocket, Mitch jerked out a couple bills and tossed them on the table. "Let's get out of here."

Curiosity filled Seth's eyes but he rose to his feet and followed Mitch out of the café.

"McAdams has some horses I'm considering buying," Mitch said, once they stood on the sidewalk. "I'd like you to see them and give me your opinion."

If Seth found the abrupt change of subject problematic, it didn't show. He glanced at his watch. "I've got an hour."

Because the McAdamses' ranch was on the way to Seth's place, they drove separately. This gave Mitch time to settle his heart and put the events in the café into proper perspective.

By the time he turned onto the long lane leading to Paul McAdams's ranch, he was prepared for any questions Seth might toss his way. He stopped in front of the barn and hopped out. Once Seth was parked, Mitch gestured toward a nearby corral.

Seth's gaze narrowed on the five horses and he covered the remaining distance in several long strides. "Are those Pryors?"

"Yep." Mitch put a foot on the bottom rail of the steel corral fence and leaned over the top. "Paul got approval to adopt these out."

Mitch had been fascinated by the free-roaming horses of the Pryor Mountains since he'd been a boy. Before he had left Montana, he had promised himself one day he'd have his own herd. Not only had he always had a soft spot in his heart for horses in general, he was determined to do his part to preserve the breed's heritage.

Seth's gaze settled on a roan that stood to the side, staring boldly at them. "That's a pretty filly."

Mitch chuckled. "Reminds me of your sister."

The words slipped from his mouth before he could stop them. Still, the way the horse stood with her head held high and her gaze so firm and direct *did* bring Anna to mind.

"Speaking of my sister," Seth said in a casual tone that Mitch suspected was anything but casual, "you never answered my question. What was that kiss about, anyway?"

Mitch found Seth's gaze fixed on the herd.

"I'm not sure," Mitch admitted now, watching the roan approach several other horses. To the casual observer, she probably appeared to be firmly ensconced in the group. But Mitch had been coming here for over a week and he'd noticed she never totally fit in.

"I thought you were dating Cassie," Seth said.

"Cassie?" The name burst from Mitch's lips, causing the horses to scatter. "Why would you think that?"

"You brought her with you to the YP event." Seth spoke confidently as if he'd given the matter some thought. "And Mrs. Barbee mentioned Cassie is always at your house."

Mitch groaned aloud. Moving in next to the pastor and his wife hadn't been the smartest choice. Still, Mitch thought Seth knew better than to believe anything coming out of Loretta Barbee's mouth. "Since when do you listen to gossip?"

"Is it true?" Seth pinned Mitch with his gaze. "Are you interested in her?"

"Of course not," Mitch snapped. "Cassie and I grew up together. She's like a sister to me. Nothing more."

For the first time since they'd walked to the corral, Seth turned and faced Mitch head-on. "How 'bout Anna? Are you interested in her?"

Interested in the prettiest blue-eyed blonde ever to come out of Sweet River? Mitch shook his head. That ship had long since sailed. He thought about offering up a simple "no way in hell" but stopped himself before the words made it past his lips.

Mitch knew Seth. Had grown up beside him. He knew if he protested too much Seth would think he was hiding something. Mitch slid his hand down the cool steel of the fence. "Your sister is an attractive woman."

Seth climbed on the rail. "C'mon, Donavan. You can do better than that."

It was time to tread lightly. He didn't want to give Seth the wrong impression. Neither did he want to lie. "Anna intrigues me. And there seems to be some chemistry between us. I noticed it at the Young Professionals meeting."

So far, so true. He'd been painfully aware of her at the meeting.

"Chemistry doesn't explain why she'd kiss you." Seth drilled him with a stare. "In such a public place."

"Impulse, evidently." Mitch shrugged. "It's hard to figure out what goes on in any woman's mind, much less one as complicated as your sister's."

"Nice save." Seth didn't look convinced, but he appeared willing to let the matter drop.

Although Mitch was grateful for the reprieve, that didn't mean he was able to stop thinking about Anna. He'd told the truth when he said she was complicated. He'd never had a clue what Anna thought about life, about her future or about him.

His gaze settled on the roan. Anna was as skittish and unpredictable as the filly in front of him. One minute she was prancing forward. The next she was practically tripping over herself as she sidestepped backward.

Anna had kissed him in public and told her brother in no uncertain terms that she'd hang out with whomever she pleased. Still, Mitch wasn't convinced she'd changed that much. But it really didn't matter. Because he had no intention of becoming emotionally involved with her...ever again.

Chapter Six

Wildflowers from the garden graced the center of Anna's dining room table. Candles strategically placed for ambience cast a golden glow. An open bottle of champagne sat in the silver bucket that had been passed down to Anna from her grandmother. When Cassie left after dropping off Stacie's wedding dress, the three roommates had decided to celebrate by having a private bridal show.

Anna lifted her flute of champagne. "To the most beautiful soon-to-be bride ever."

"It's the dress." A dusky rose blush stole its way up Stacie's neck and across her cheeks. "Cassie did an amazing job."

The floor-length, white, satin-and-lace gown was

the perfect dress for such a wondrous occasion. With its wide neckline and lace waistband with scallops, the romantic dress was made to fulfill a princess's dreams of the most important day of her life.

Lauren placed her glass on the sideboard of Anna's dining room then rested her hand on Stacie's lace-covered shoulder. "The dress is lovely. *You* are gorgeous."

"I've never been happier." Stacie's gaze dropped to the platinum-set solitaire on her left hand. "I can't believe in a few weeks, I'll be Josh's wife."

Anna could scarcely believe it herself. When the three friends had come to Sweet River four months ago, the plan was to stay only long enough for Lauren to get the data needed for her dissertation research. Then they'd return to their lives in Denver. But Stacie had fallen in love and decided to make her life here.

The wedding was to be a small, intimate afternoon affair in the old house that had been home to them since their arrival. A dance open to the community would follow that evening at the civic center.

"I can't wait to see our bridesmaids' dresses." Anna found herself getting caught up in the excitement filling the air. "Lauren and I are stopping by Cassie's house on Saturday for the final fitting."

"Cassie said your dresses are really pretty." Stacie took a sip of champagne and a dreamy look filled her gaze. "You're going to be fighting off every cowboy from a three-county area at the dance."

Lauren laughed then quickly sobered. "There aren't many cowboys interested in a clinical psychologist."

"All it takes is one," Stacie said mysteriously before turning to Anna. "How about you? Think there's a cowboy in your future?"

Anna shoved aside the image of Mitch in nothing but a Stetson. "Um, no."

The words had barely left her mouth when a pair of headlights turned from the street into the drive. The rumble of the engine stilled and the lights shut off. A second later the sound of a car door slamming could be heard through the closed windows.

Anna turned back to her friends. "Either of you expecting company?"

Stacie shook her head. Lauren, who was closest to the window, stepped forward and pushed back the lace curtains with one hand. "Looks like Josh's truck."

A delighted smile followed quickly by panic skittered across Stacie's face. "He can't see me in the dress," she wailed. "It's bad luck."

At first Anna wasn't sure how to respond. The remark seemed more suited to a woman of her Grandma Borghild's generation than her thoroughly modern roommate. But when she realized Stacie was serious, Anna gave her friend a gentle shove. "Go upstairs. I'll see what he wants."

"Tell him I love him." Stacie hiked up her skirts and ran up the stairs with Lauren following behind with the train.

The doorbell chimed just as the two women disappeared from view. By the time Anna reached the foyer, the melody began again.

"Hold on. I'm coming." Anna's heels clacked, clacked, clacked against the hardwood. She hoped Josh would understand why he couldn't see his fiancée this evening.

Not only because of the dress but because tonight had been specifically set aside as a girls' night. This was her and Lauren's chance to ooh and aah over Stacie's wedding dress. The opportunity to enjoy it being just the three of them for a little while longer. The realization that this might be one of the *last* times Anna would enjoy such closeness with her friends brought a lump to her throat.

She shook aside the melancholy thought and eased open the heavy oak door, a greeting for Josh on her lips. But instead of one man, Anna found herself facing a triple threat. Seth, Josh and Mitch stood on the porch, their broad shoulders an impenetrable wall.

Anna hadn't seen Mitch since the incident in the café two days ago. The kiss had been an impulsive gesture in response to a dare. The aftermath had been anything but simple.

The whole town was buzzing. Norm at the café had started taking bets on when she and Mitch would walk down the aisle. It was rumored Mrs. Barbee had reserved the church for the June date she'd picked.

And it wasn't just the townsfolk reading too much into a kiss. Her own friends hadn't believed she'd been merely responding to a dare. But she'd forgiven them. They didn't know how susceptible she was to Mitch, er, to a dare.

"Earth to Anna."

Her brother's teasing tone brought Anna back to reality with a jolt.

"Hey, guys." Anna's greeting was directed to all three but when she placed a hand against the door frame, she focused only on Seth. "What can I do for you?"

He glanced at the arm blocking his entrance. "Well, for starters you can be a good hostess and invite us in."

"No can do." While Anna didn't truly believe it was bad luck for the groom to see his bride in her dress before the wedding, Stacie believed it. That was what mattered.

"Why not— Oh, of course." Seth stepped back, the look on his face reminding Anna of the time he'd dropped a mouse down the front of her dress. "You want to give Mitch a welcome smooch first."

Anna watched in horror as her brother gestured toward Mitch. "He's right here. Go ahead. Plant one on him. It's not like you haven't done it before."

Josh chuckled.

Mitch's open hand slapped Seth's back. "Cut it out, Anderssen."

Anna fixed a hard glare on her brother. His innocent expression didn't fool her in the least. After a moment she shifted her gaze to Stacie's fiancé. "The reason you can't come in is because Stacie is trying on her wedding dress."

Josh tilted his head and stared as if she was speaking a foreign language. "I won't stay long."

Anna had always liked Josh. Liked the way he treated Stacie. Liked the way his eyes softened whenever she was near. Far be it from her to stand between two lovers, but this time it couldn't be helped. "It's bad luck for the groom to see the bride in her dress before the wedding."

A startled look swept across Josh's face. "Seriously?"

Anna nodded. "It's an old wives' tale but Stacie believes it. She ran up the stairs when she saw your truck in the drive."

Josh cast a questioning glance at his friends.

"Lots of women believe that," Seth confirmed. "It's just one more thing for them to stress about."

Mitch raised his hands when Josh's gaze settled on him. "Don't ask me."

Josh turned back to Anna. "The last thing I want to do is add to her stress."

Anna's admiration for Josh inched up another notch.

After a moment he reached into his pocket and pulled out a small silver phone. "This is her new cell. I took the old one to the store in Billings today, but they said it wasn't worth repairing. Would you give it to her?"

"Certainly." Anna took the phone and offered him a warm smile. "I almost forgot. Stacie said to tell you she loves you."

She started to shut the door but Seth's boot shot out and blocked it from closing.

"Not so fast, baby sister," Seth said. "Mitch and I have something to discuss with you."

Anna dug her nails into her palm. The last thing she wanted was a brother-sister chat with Seth.

"Like I said, I'm busy this evening." Anna tried for

calm and matter-of-fact but she could hear a slight tremor in her voice.

"It has nothing to do with what happened in the café," Mitch said in a low tone.

For the first time since she'd opened the door, Anna really looked at Mitch. She immediately realized her mistake. The blue of his eyes. The stubble on his cheeks. And the tangy scent she remembered so well. Her heart skipped a beat.

"This is important, Anna. It'll only take a few minutes. Mitch is going fishing this weekend and he doesn't have any gear." Seth spoke quickly as if he realized his time was running out. "I promised him he could use Grandpa's."

Anna turned to Mitch. "You like to fish?"

He smiled at her surprise. "For as long as I can remember."

That meant he'd been a fishing fanatic when they'd been together. Yet in the three months they'd "dated," they'd never sat by a stream nor taken a picnic lunch to the penny pond.

Because I couldn't chance anyone seeing us.

Regret for what might have been washed over her. She stepped to the side. "The tackle box is in the furnace room."

"Don't forget to give the phone to Stacie." Josh met Anna's gaze. "I hate to think of her being on the road without a cell."

"No worries." Anna touched his arm and realized how lucky her friend was to be so loved.

"I'll keep Josh company out here," Mitch said to Seth.

Seth shrugged. "This won't take long, anyway."

Anna shifted her gaze to Josh and Mitch. "Can I get you two a glass of champagne while you're waiting?"

"Make it a beer and you're on," Josh said.

"Same for me," Mitch said.

"Back in a flash." Anna returned several minutes later and found the men sitting around the wicker table on the porch talking…horses. She tried to be unobtrusive but Mitch looked up when she approached the table with the bottles.

"You look pretty this evening," Mitch said when she handed him a bottle. "The dress suits you."

Anna flushed with pleasure at the compliment. If her friends had liked the black and tan dress she'd designed herself, they hadn't mentioned it.

She wasn't surprised Mitch had commented. He'd always been observant and quick to compliment. That long-ago summer she'd accepted his admiration as her due. Not once had she taken the time to give him the attention *he* deserved.

Of course, it wasn't all her fault. She'd never known what made him tick. He'd never talked much about himself or shared his feelings. Anna realized that was part of what had made her so insecure. She hadn't even been shocked when she'd called him a month after they'd broken up to find he'd already hopped back into the dating scene. She'd always suspected he could walk away from her without a second thought.

After seeing him tonight, she realized how easy it would be to fall into old habits. To believe there was something between them other than sexual chemistry.

History had taught her the dangers of falling in love with Mitch Donavan. She'd be foolish not to heed the lesson.

Chapter Seven

"I absolutely adore it." Lauren gazed into the full-length mirror Cassie had set up in her living room. "You did a fabulous job on this dress."

Anna slid her hand down the smooth black satin. Lauren was right. The cocktail-length bridesmaids' dresses were surprisingly flattering. "You have real talent."

Cassie looked up from where she was pinning the hem of Lauren's dress and smiled. "It's not a job for me or just a way to earn money. Sewing is my passion."

"That's what Stacie says about her cooking," Anna said. "Only she calls it her 'bliss.'"

"I feel that way when I finish a counseling session." A warmth, a richness, filled Lauren's voice. "I'm happy. Satisfied. Honored that someone trusts me enough to share their innermost thoughts."

Anna nodded absently, unable to pull her gaze from the mirror. Edged in walnut and beveled, the mirror was a twin of the one she'd stood in front of so many times as a young teen. A former beauty queen, her mother had taken Anna's pageants very seriously. The prettiest dress had never been good enough. *And I'd never been good enough, either....*

Even after all these years, the realization still filled her with sadness.

"What about you, Anna?" Cassie prompted. "What's your passion?"

"Growing up, I wanted to be a teacher. I love kids." A familiar heaviness pulled at Anna's heart, making it difficult for her to breathe. "But when I got to college that changed. Fashion merchandising and design became my passion."

"You never told me you wanted to be a teacher." The words had barely left Lauren's mouth when the front door flew open and two gangly boys burst through the front door.

"Mo-om," the taller one bellowed without even glancing around.

"You won't believe what I—" The younger of the two stopped when he saw his mother wasn't alone. Both boys held fishing rods.

The older one stopped in his tracks, his gaze skipping past Lauren and Anna to settle on his mother. A look of disappointment crossed his face. "I didn't know you had friends over."

Cassie made quick work of the introductions, her pride in the boys evident in her tone. Anna learned the taller one with a mop of blond hair was thirteen-year-old Trenton. Ten-year-old Brandon had dark hair like his mother and was the one blushing furiously when his mother made him shake hands.

"Now take those poles and put them in the garage, please," Cassie said in a motherly tone. "You know they don't belong in the house."

"What about the fish?" An amused voice sounded from the doorway. "Can I bring *them* inside?"

Anna recognized the voice immediately. Her heart flip-flopped. She hadn't seen Mitch since Wednesday when he'd stopped by her house with Seth and Josh.

In worn jeans and a gray sweatshirt, he was dressed more casually than he'd been that night. But even his attire and five o'clock shadow didn't detract from his attractiveness. Mitch had always been the most handsome man she'd ever known. And the most sexy.

A heat stole over Anna that had nothing to do with the number of people now occupying the small living room. And when her gaze lingered on his lips, she experienced an overwhelming urge to kiss him again.

Because that option was totally unworkable, Anna jerked her gaze from his mouth and settled it on the string of catfish instead.

"I caught three of 'em myself," Brandon proudly announced.

Mitch smiled at the younger boy's enthusiasm as he rested a hand on the older boy's shoulder. "You've got two good fishermen."

Trenton shrugged off the praise, but Anna could see how much the words meant to him.

Mitch would make a good father.

The thought came out of nowhere, rekindling the ache in Anna's heart.

"Thanks for taking them, Mitch. It's nice for them to have a guy to hang out with." Cassie crossed the room and took the string of fish from his hand. "I hope you're still planning to stay for dinner."

Mitch hesitated, his gaze taking in Anna and Lauren in their pinned-up dresses. "Looks like you have your hands full right now. We can do it another time."

"Don't let us interfere with your date." The tightness gripping Anna's chest was at odds with her casual tone. "We're just finishing up here."

"It's not a date," Mitch said slowly and distinctly. "Just a fish fry."

Cassie's smile froze. "Mitch is correct. It's just fish and my sour cream and dill potato salad."

"I don't like potato salad," Trenton said. "Neither does Brandon."

"Well, *I* like it," Mitch said.

Cassie shot him a grateful smile.

"We went to the penny pond," Brandon said. "I threw in ten pennies. Trenton said I was stupid."

"You called your brother *stupid?*" Cassie's gaze settled on her oldest son and Trenton visibly squirmed.

"I didn't say *he* was stupid." Trenton shot his brother a glare.

"Thank goodn—" Cassie began.

"You did so," Brandon insisted.

"I said throwing the pennies in the pond was stupid," Trenton clarified.

"Pennies in a pond?" Lauren's expression was clearly puzzled.

"It's a tradition around here," Anna explained. "If you make a wish when you toss one in, the wish is supposed to come true."

"Don't tell me people actually believe that—" Lauren stopped at Brandon's crestfallen expression.

"There are lots of people around here who swear by it." Anna nodded her head for extra emphasis.

"That's why I threw them in," Brandon said, an earnest expression on his young face.

"You don't believe in that stuff, do you?" Trenton's gaze pinned Mitch.

"There's a few of my pennies in the bottom of that pond," Mitch said.

"Yeah, but did your wish come true?" Trenton pressed.

Was Anna only imagining it or did Mitch look at her before he answered?

"Some did." He shrugged. "The jury is still out on the others."

Trenton cocked his head back. "Huh?"

"He means that while some haven't come true yet, they still may," Cassie explained to her son, even as her gaze remained fixed on Mitch.

"Like buying the building downtown?" Cassie asked Mitch.

Mitch paused for a moment then nodded. "Exactly."

Anna experienced a surge of disappointment but wasn't sure why.

"What about the fish?" Brandon tugged at Mitch's sleeve. "You promised I could help you cook 'em."

"I did," Mitch said. "And you will."

His response didn't surprise Anna. For as long as she'd known him, his word had been his bond. That was why her betrayal had been so significant. He'd grown up surrounded by people whose word meant nothing.

His mother had promised to take care of him, yet she'd died when Mitch had been about Trenton's age. Worse yet, she'd left him with a father who had difficulty taking care of himself, much less a growing boy.

"I'd really like it if you'd both join us for supper." Cassie's voice broke through Anna's thoughts. "A little more estrogen in this house would do us all good."

"Huh?" Brandon said, his expression clearly puzzled.

"It's a woman thing," Mitch said to the boy.

Brandon's brows drew together. "But what's estro—"

"I'll explain later." Cassie offered her son a smile before shifting her gaze back to Anna and Lauren. "You'll stay, won't you?"

"I'm afraid I can't." Regret filled Lauren's voice. "I have a client coming in—" She glanced at the thin gold watch on her wrist and gasped. "—thirty minutes."

"A client?" Anna couldn't keep the surprise from her voice. Although Lauren had mentioned several times that she missed counseling, she'd never said she had a *client*. "Since when?"

"Last-minute thing," Lauren said with an apologetic smile. "But if you want to stay for dinner, go ahead. Actually it'd probably work out better if you weren't there when she arrives."

Thoroughly confused, Anna could only stare.

"I don't know this young woman, but you may," Lauren explained. "She might not want you knowing she's coming for counseling."

"No worries," Anna said. "I'll stay away."

"We'd better get the fish cleaned and ready for the skillet." Though Mitch's polite smile encompassed both Lauren and Anna, his gaze seemed to linger a heartbeat longer on Anna. "Good to see you again."

His duty done, Mitch herded the boys from the room while Lauren disappeared into the bedroom to change. Moments later Brandon reappeared in the doorway.

"Mitch says I'm in charge of setting the table." His chest puffed out with pride. "Are your friends staying?"

"I understand Lauren has to leave but I'd really like it if you'd stay." Cassie reached over and touched Anna's arm. "I'll give you a ride home."

Anna hesitated. She knew the invitation was sincere but there was Mitch to consider. This was his evening with Cassie and the boys. The last thing she wanted was for him to feel as if she were being crammed down his throat. "I don't want to intrude."

"Mitch," Cassie called out before she could even finish the thought. "Anna thinks you don't want her to stay."

"Cassie." Anna clenched her fists, resisting the urge to throttle her friend.

Mitch stuck his head through the doorway, his gaze swiveling immediately to Anna. "Why would you think that?"

To his credit, he appeared genuinely perplexed.

"Cassie misunderstood my hesitation," Anna said.

"If that's not the reason, then what is?" Cassie's topaz-colored eyes clouded with confusion.

Why was Cassie being so obtuse? For a brief moment, Anna was tempted to lie, but the words wouldn't come. She'd promised herself she'd be honest…with herself and with others. By God, she was going to stick to that promise.

"If you must know," Anna said, feeling her confidence in the rightness of her decision grow with each word, "I didn't want to be a third wheel."

Mitch and Cassie exchanged confused glances.

"C'mon, you guys," Anna said. "Everyone knows that when a couple is first dating, they don't want another person around."

Cassie sucked in an audible breath.

"What?" The word shot from Mitch's lips and shattered on the wall behind Anna. "You think Cassie and I are *dating?*"

A weaker woman might have backed down. Anna lifted her chin. "You're together all the time."

"She lives down the block," Mitch said. "We're just good friends. Isn't that right, Cass?"

Was it only Anna's imagination or did Cassie hesitate ever so slightly?

"Absolutely," Cassie said with a firm nod.

Mitch took several steps toward Anna. His gaze fused with hers. "Don't go."

The air grew thick. A curious thrumming filled Anna's veins. Her lips began to tingle....

"Are you staying or not?" Brandon's question shattered the connection.

"I am." Anna forced a calm she didn't feel. "Set another place at the table."

Mitch stared down at his half-empty plate, amazed he'd managed to eat anything at all. The freshly fried fish had tasted like boot leather and he'd had no appetite for Cassie's blue-ribbon potato salad.

All because of Anna.

She hadn't sat next to him, or even directly across from him, but he'd been aware of her presence throughout the entire meal. And every time she spoke, he'd been reminded that she was only there because he'd asked her to stay.

It had been an arrogant and extremely foolish move. He'd wanted to prove to himself that he was immune. To prove that as far as he was concerned, she was just another woman. To prove that what they'd shared all those years ago was totally in the past.

The problem was he hadn't factored in the chemistry. Even when he wasn't talking directly to her, he couldn't help being aware of her. The twinkle that lit her blue eyes when she'd asked the boys if they had girlfriends. The flush in her cheeks when Trenton had turned the table and asked if she had a boyfriend. The pain in his gut when she'd said she didn't have time for one.

Not because he wanted her to have a boyfriend. Or because, God forbid, *he* wanted to be her boyfriend. No, he'd been disappointed because, well, it showed that she was as self-centered as ever.

Knowing that, he still desired her.

Mitch dropped his fork to the plate, the realization stabbing like a red-hot branding iron. Even after all these years, after the history between them, he'd never gotten over her.

He thought he'd moved on but he now realized he'd kept one boot in the past. It helped explain why he hadn't been able to find and form a lasting relationship.

I've never gotten Anna Anderssen out of my system.

He vividly remembered the split. Up to that point, all had been good. When he'd seen her at the celebration, he'd felt as if he'd hit a brick wall going sixty. For almost thirteen years, that had been the last he'd seen of her.

She'd called once, maybe a month or so after he'd returned to college. He'd been out on a date but missing her something fierce.

Despite his anger, when she said she wanted to talk, he'd almost ditched his date. But unlike his father,

Mitch had stayed strong. Not only hadn't he taken his date home, he'd done the gentlemanly thing and gotten off the phone as soon as possible.

Anna had never called him again.

"Did I tell you that I saw your dad when I was in Billings yesterday?" Cassie asked, forking a bite of fish.

Mitch shifted his gaze to Anna. "I thought your folks were in Florida."

"They are," Anna said. "I think Cassie's talking about your dad, not mine."

Del was in Montana? Mitch shot a glance at Cassie. A sick feeling filled the pit of his stomach at her nod. He swallowed hard. "He's alive?"

When Cassie nodded again, Mitch didn't know whether to be relieved or disappointed. Since his father had left Sweet River all those years ago, Mitch hadn't heard from him. He'd assumed his old man had drowned in a bottle of whiskey.

Delbert Donavan had been a weak and desperately unhappy man. The day Mitch turned eighteen his dad left him and Sweet River behind.

"We didn't get much of a chance to talk," Cassie said.

"How did he seem?" Anna asked.

Mitch knew what Anna was really asking. Had his father been lying in some gutter when Cassie had seen him? Had he been coherent enough to recognize her? Had he even asked about his son?

Though Mitch found himself listening intently for Cassie's response, he didn't really care if Del was alive or dead, sober or drunk. As far as he was concerned, his father, like Anna, was his past. And it was a past he had no intention of revisiting.

Chapter Eight

"Watch out." Alex jerked Anna back from the curb.

A Jeep filled with laughing teenagers whizzed by. So close Anna could hear the song playing on the car stereo. So close she could feel the air whoosh past her. So close she could see the startled expression on the faces of the passengers.

Her heart slammed against her ribs. If she hadn't met Alex on her way to the civic center, she would probably be lying in the street right now…hurt, bleeding or even worse.

"Buckets of blood," Anna swore, her voice high-pitched and breathless. "I don't know how I didn't see it."

"They were going too fast." A muscle in Alex's jaw

jumped. "John Redmond's boy was driving. If I see the sheriff tonight, he'll hear about this."

Anna took calming breaths. After several seconds her heart resumed its normal rhythm. Though she agreed Kyle Redmond needed to slow down, it was too beautiful a night for anger. The air was crisp, but not cold and the smell of dried leaves filled the air.

"We'd better get going or we'll be late." Anna hoped her cheery tone would lift Alex's suddenly dark mood.

"I don't care if you agree or not." His fingers tightened on her arm. "I'm going to talk to the sheriff."

"You'll have your chance." Carefully looking both ways, Anna stepped off the curb. With his hand still on her arm, she left Alex little choice but to follow. The heels of her boots clicked against the concrete as they crossed Main Street. She breathed a sigh of relief when she reached the other side and stepped safely onto the sidewalk. "Everyone in Sweet River will be at the center tonight—including the sheriff."

The annual community soup supper had grown so popular that the civic center was the only place where it could be held. The wide samplings of soups and chili, not to mention the plethora of specialty breads and baked goods, added to the event's appeal.

"I heard Stacie is making the soups this year," Alex said in a conversational tone.

"She's in charge of the kitchen." Anna couldn't keep the pride from her voice. In the four months since Stacie had come to Sweet River, her friend had become an integral part of the community.

Alex slowed his pace to accommodate her heels. "You look very pretty this evening."

The unexpected compliment brought a smile to her face. She'd deemed the pumpkin-colored skirt and sweater perfect for a fall event. Her boots dressed down the outfit enough to make it suitable for a small-town soup supper.

"You're looking pretty hot yourself," Anna countered.

Alex had chosen gray wool pants, a navy sweater and Italian loafers. Many women would find him attractive. It still surprised her that she didn't feel the slightest tingle when he was close.

"Isn't that Cassie and Mitch?" The words had barely left his mouth when Alex dropped his hand from Anna's arm and sprinted ahead.

After a few seconds of trying to keep up, Anna slowed her steps. After all, it wasn't as if she and Alex were going to the event together. And she cringed at the thought of giving the appearance of chasing Mitch.

Alex didn't appear to notice she was no longer beside him. Once he closed in on Mitch and Cassie, Anna slowed her pace even more. She paused and checked out the new autumn display in a store window, using the time to rid herself of the green-eyed monster who had her heart in a stranglehold and wouldn't let go.

Seeing Mitch with Cassie shouldn't have disturbed her. Who he saw, who he *dated* was none of her business. And really, her feelings were probably more surprise than jealousy. After all, last weekend he'd told her that he and Cassie were just friends. Yet here they were, together again.

Anna pressed her lips tight. For a couple who weren't a couple, they certainly were spending a lot of time hanging out. If Mitch liked Cassie as more than a friend, he should just be honest and say so.

"Could you walk any slower?"

Anna jerked her head up at Alex's teasing tone and blinked.

The young attorney, flanked by Mitch and Cassie, stood smack-dab in front of her, blocking her path.

"You didn't have to wait on me," Anna protested to Alex.

"Of course I did," Alex said in a loud, hearty voice. "When we ran into each other, we said we'd walk to the event together."

It could have been a coincidence that in one sentence Alex had made it perfectly clear that while Anna had been with him, they weren't *really* together. Which was good—but surprising—given the fact Alex had made it clear he'd like to date her. Before she could respond, Alex and Mitch started down the sidewalk talking about The Hattan.

"I thought you'd be helping Stacie in the kitchen tonight." Cassie fell into step beside Anna on a sidewalk just wide enough for two.

"I volunteered, but Josh and Lauren beat me to it." There was no need to mention that once Anna had heard Loretta Barbee was in charge of the event, her desire to participate had vanished. "I decided to support the supper by enjoying the food."

"With Alex?" Cassie asked.

Though Cassie hadn't spoken in a particularly loud tone and Mitch didn't break stride, Anna had the feeling he was listening.

"Like he said, we ran into each other on the way," Anna said. "Why do you ask?"

"No reason. Just curious." Cassie immediately changed the subject to the bridesmaids' dresses.

Anna listened to her friend talk, murmuring appropriate words every now and then. With each step, she became more keenly aware of Mitch, barely a foot in front of her. His jeans, long-sleeved cotton shirt and boots might be more casual than Alex's designer attire, but in her estimation, he'd never looked better. And he smelled plenty good, too. The intoxicating scent of his cologne teased her nostrils and sent desire coursing through her veins.

By the time they reached the civic center's front door, which Mitch pulled open for her, Anna felt slightly tipsy.

Alex glanced around the large community hall filled with tables. "How about we all sit together?"

"Maybe we should split up and mingle." Anna forced a smile that felt overly bright. "That might be fun."

Though she felt like a coward for wanting to keep her distance from Mitch, it was self-preservation. Ten minutes of close proximity and she'd discovered that her control wasn't nearly as strong as it had been "BK," before the kiss.

"I'm afraid that's not going to happen," Loretta Barbee interjected in a tone that was pleasant, yet firm. "There's assigned seating tonight."

Looking elegant in blue chiffon, the pastor's wife sat behind a table with what looked like red raffle tickets in front of her.

"We've never been told where to sit before." Anna attempted to keep her tone equally pleasant but failed.

Loretta met Anna's challenging tone with one of her own. "Anna, my dear, you've been away a long time. We went to specified seating quite a ways back. This year—as the event chairperson—I decided to mix things up. Everyone gets a number and that's where they sit. It's a way to get to know more people in the community…and like you said, to encourage folks to mingle."

Although it was what she'd wished for, Anna experienced a feeling of foreboding. Loretta's eyes were too bright, her tone too cheery and the smile lifting her red lips almost a smirk.

"Sounds like a good idea to me," Cassie said enthusiastically, apparently not feeling the same hesitation.

"From a business perspective, it never hurts to meet new people," Alex agreed.

Mitch remained silent. The stiffness in his shoulders told Anna she wasn't the only one with misgivings.

"Now that we've got that settled, let me give you

your seating assignments," Loretta said. "We have tables of eight, four and a few for two. The ticket I'll give you will have your table number printed on it."

"Seems complicated for a simple soup supper," Mitch muttered.

Anna hid a smile.

"Here are your tickets." Loretta handed one to Alex and one to Cassie.

Cassie glanced down. "I'm table eight."

Alex's eyes brightened and he held up his ticket. "We're together."

"Is that okay with you?" Cassie's brows pulled together in a worried frown. "I know you were hoping to network tonight."

"No exchanges." Loretta didn't even attempt to pretend she wasn't listening.

"I've also been hoping for a chance to get to know you better," Alex said gallantly, his attention focused completely on Cassie.

A hint of pink cut a swath across her cheeks. She shifted her gaze to Anna and Mitch. "Maybe you'll be at our table, too."

"Here you go, my dear." Loretta placed a ticket in Anna's hand before giving one to Mitch. "Remember. No switching."

A large, rowdy group from Millstead's, a nearby dude ranch, came through the doors, pushing Anna and Mitch forward. Loretta jumped to her feet, sputtering like a wet hen when the group tried to bypass the registration table.

"Where is your seat?" Cassie asked as they stepped to the side.

Mitch's gaze dropped to the small red ticket. "Fourteen."

Anna shifted her attention to her own ticket. She nearly groaned out loud. No wonder Loretta had looked so smug.

"What does yours say?" Alex peered over her shoulder.

"Fourteen." Anna found her irritation at Loretta's oh-so-obvious attempt to throw her at Mitch laced with a trace of excitement.

"Too bad we couldn't all be together," Cassie said. "Yet, with so many at each table I'm sure we'll all get lots of mingling."

"Unless we decide we'd rather talk to the person next to us," Alex said with an unexpected wink.

Cassie blushed and sashayed past him, a pleased smile hovering on her lips.

The two had barely left when a hand settled on Mitch's shoulder. Resplendent in dark pants, a crisp white shirt and steer-head bolo tie, Henry Millstead, owner of the largest dude ranch in the area, offered Mitch a hearty smile.

"Mitchell, I didn't expect to see you here tonight." Henry's gaze shifted from Mitch to Anna. "And with such a beautiful lady."

Anna smiled and held out her hand. "I don't know if you remember me."

"Of course I remember you. Tom and Dottie's girl,

Anna." Henry's smile filled with engaging warmth. "You growed up real nice."

"Yes, she did." Mitch nodded.

Anna felt warmth spread up her neck.

"I spoke with your father last week," Henry said. "Sounds like he's keeping himself busy."

"He loves Florida," Anna said. "I know he thinks Seth and I are crazy for living where it snows."

"Life in Montana isn't for everyone," Henry agreed. "When Mitch left, the wife and I worried he might like big-city life so much he'd never move back."

"I couldn't stay away," Mitch said. "Not from you and Marg. You're the only family I have."

Anna couldn't imagine what it was like for Mitch, knowing a former employer cared more for him than his own dad.

"Take your seats, everyone." Loretta's loud voice, at odds with her small stature, rang out over the conversational din.

"The Queen has spoken," Henry said with a grin. But instead of leaving, he turned back to Mitch. "We'd like to see you at the ranch more."

"I'll call Marg and set something up," Mitch said.

"Hell," Henry's voice boomed. "You don't need to call. Just stop out. Anytime." He shifted his gaze to Anna. "You, too, missy. Don't be a stranger."

After Anna promised, Henry left to find his table.

"I'm going to see where we're sitting," Anna told Mitch. She took off through the crowd, not even looking back to see if he was following. "Here it is."

It was number fourteen, a small linen-clad table positioned next to a fake ficus tree.

She felt Mitch behind her and turned. "There are only two seats."

He grinned unexpectedly. "Think about who made the assignments."

Anna chuckled. "She did look rather pleased with herself."

"Pleased with herself?" Mitch laughed. "The woman was practically orgasmic."

The word conjured up all sorts of images. None of them appropriate for a church-sponsored soup supper.

Mitch pulled out her chair. "This is going to keep the gossips talking for weeks."

"They do love to speculate," Anna said, sliding into the seat.

"I'd almost forgotten how much." Mitch moved to the other side of the table, pulled out the chair and then sat down. His gaze dropped to the menu on the table. After a moment, he looked up. "Which soup are you going to have?"

Good. He was at least attempting to keep their interaction more businesslike than personal. Anna exhaled a sigh of relief. Perhaps getting through supper with Loretta's beady bird eyes on them was going to be easier than she thought.

Mitch knew what he wanted, and after some hemming and hawing, Anna came to a decision. By the time he returned to the table with a tray filled with a bowl of chili with all the toppings for him, and Gouda cheese soup for her, Loretta had already been by to personally drop off a basket of assorted breads.

"Loretta stopped by," Anna informed him when he grabbed a square of corn bread with jalapeños from the basket. "She wanted to know what I thought of the table."

He lifted a brow. "What did you tell her?"

"I said it was nice and told her the ficus tree with the white lights added to the ambience." Anna could tell that answer wasn't the one Loretta had been expecting. "I made sure she knew that I thought it was the nicest table in the whole room."

"I bet that really got her going." Mitch slathered butter onto the corn bread. "Was she twittering?"

"Twittering?"

"You know," he said. "Barely able to get the words out. Surely you've noticed she twitters when she gets flustered."

Anna laughed. What she *had* noticed was that she was having an absolutely delightful conversation with Mitch. "She also asked if I thought Cassie was upset because I was with you."

That question had thrown her. Anna knew the pastor's wife was betting Anna would end up with Mitch. That was why her attempt to stir things up made so little sense.

"That surprises me." Mitch shook his head. "I was positive she knew how much Cassie liked Alex."

"Like?" Anna straightened in her chair. "As in boyfriend-girlfriend like?"

Mitch shrugged. "All I know is earlier this evening Cassie told me she thought Alex was good-looking and hoped to get to know him better."

Anna could hear Cassie saying the words but she wasn't convinced they were true. She'd seen the way Cassie looked at Mitch. It wouldn't surprise her if the pretty brunette had made the comment hoping to make Mitch jealous.

"Despite Loretta's machinations, it all worked out in the end," Mitch added, matching Alex's earlier gallantry.

"You don't mind sitting with me?" Anna asked, feeling like a schoolgirl wrangling for a compliment.

"Of course not." Mitch shot her a smile, the kind she'd seen frequently that long-ago summer. One that still turned her bones to jelly. "What man doesn't want to spend time with a pretty girl?"

A wave of warmth washed over Anna. He'd been such a gentleman about the apology, the kiss and now, being stuck with her for the evening.

"I'm sorry about the kiss." Anna dropped her gaze to the smooth surface of her soup. "I didn't mean to stir up gossip."

He waved away her apology. "I'm just curious why you did it."

"You dared—"

"Why did you really do it?" he repeated, dumping a handful of crackers into his chili. There was no anger in his voice, no irritation in his tone, only curiosity.

Anna thought back to that moment. Despite her best efforts, she felt her cheeks warm.

"Because I wanted to," she mumbled.

"What?" The corn bread slipped from his fingers and landed upside down on the plate. "I'm not sure I heard correctly."

Anna briefly considered playing coy but discarded the option. Instead she lifted her chin and met his gaze head-on. "I kissed you because I wanted to. Don't even try to tell me you don't feel the magnetic pull."

Mitch laid his spoon on the table. "Of course I feel it."

Relief sluiced through her. "The sizzle was still there for you, too."

He chuckled. "You can say that again."

"I've never found that heat with anyone else." Anna picked up a biscuit and forced a nonchalant tone. "Have you?"

"Nope," he said, just as matter-of-factly, biting into the corn bread.

Anna took a bite from one of Stacie's famous buttermilk biscuits, but barely tasted it. Though her head had more red flags popping up than a shooting booth at an arcade, she gazed up at Mitch through lowered lashes and continued to play with fire. "Any theories on why that is?"

Mitch shrugged. "Does it matter?"

"It *does* matter." Anna leaned forward, resting her elbows on the table. "I've dated quite a bit since high school, but no one special. Sometimes I feel that I was left with too-high expectations. We burned hot and bright the entire time we were together, like one of those comets that streak across the sky. But then, instead of burning out naturally, we came to an abrupt halt."

She'd said more than she'd planned to, but the fact was that particularly over the past ten years, every time a relationship ended, she'd thought long and hard about what went wrong. But she'd never been able to pinpoint the problem. Until now.

"You might be onto something," Mitch said.

"Until I figure out a way to get you out of my system, I think I'm doomed to have unhappy relationships," Anna said with a sigh.

"How is everything this evening?" Though she'd already been by once, Loretta stood tableside again, her eyes brimming with curiosity.

"The chili was very good." Mitch pushed back his chair and abruptly stood. "But Anna and I need to be going."

"You're leaving?" A look of genuine distress crossed the older woman's face. "The Sweet Adelines are still tuning up."

Anna hurried to her feet. She wasn't sure what Mitch was up to but if it involved getting away from Loretta Barbee's scrutiny, she was game.

"It's business." Anna made a great show of looking at her watch. "We'd better hurry or we'll be late."

"Business." Loretta sniffed. "More like monkey business."

The last few words were low but still audible. As Mitch moved to her side, Anna was seized with an overwhelming urge to giggle.

They were almost to the door when Anna nudged Mitch. "Got some 'monkey business' in mind, cowboy?"

Mitch grinned. "Guess you'll have to wait and see."

Out of the corner of her eye, Anna caught a glimpse of Cassie laughing with Alex. She stopped abruptly, wondering how she could have been so thoughtless.

"What's the matter?" Mitch asked.

"You came with Cassie."

"We came together because we're neighbors, not because we're on a date." He glanced over. A look of satisfaction crossed his face when Cassie leaned close and whispered something in Alex's ear. "She's with the man she wants to walk her home."

Still Anna hesitated. "Are you sure?"

Mitch reached past her to open the door. "Trust me." He slipped an arm around her shoulders. "I know exactly what I'm doing."

Chapter Nine

Had he really asked her to trust him? That was asking a lot, considering Mitch didn't even trust himself. Nor did he have the slightest clue what he was doing.

When she'd started talking about the past, it had gotten him remembering. Being with her *had* been like riding a red-hot comet. He'd never come close to that level of intensity with any woman since. Her theory on the hazards of "love interrupted" had made a surprising amount of sense.

If they'd had a "normal" relationship, he might have been more realistic when it came to his expectations of other women. Instead of looking for that same level of intensity, perhaps he'd have understood that boring was sometimes normal.

As he walked down the sidewalk with the sweet scent of Anna's perfume wafting in the air, Mitch noted the direction of his thoughts and it scared him. He told himself to put an immediate stop to such craziness.

"I have a proposition for you," he found himself saying instead.

Anna stumbled over a crack in the sidewalk and he reached out a steadying hand. A lightning bolt of heat shot up his arm. At that moment he knew his course was set.

"What kind of proposition?"

"We should start dating," he said in as controlled a tone as he could muster. "It's the only way we'll be able to put the past behind us."

He'd initially considered asking her to come home with him, but discarded that option with great reluctance. Sex, no matter how great, wouldn't be enough to purge Anna from his system.

Anna abruptly stopped walking and paused at the entrance to a neighborhood park. Without saying a word, she pushed open the black wrought-iron gate and stepped inside. "I need a few minutes to think."

The light from an ornate lamppost cast a golden glow over the swings and merry-go-round, giving it a surreal feel. Or perhaps the surreal quality came from being there with Anna.

A tiny smile lifted the corners of her lips as her gaze settled on the swings. "I loved coming here when I was a kid."

She took the closest swing and Mitch sat down in the rubber U-shaped one next to hers.

"A park doesn't seem your kind of place." Mitch twisted in his swing to face her. "Too dirty."

Anna's brows pulled together. "Dirty?"

Mitch could tell by her tone that he'd offended her. That hadn't been his intent at all. In fact he'd meant it as a compliment. "You've always been so neat and clean. Even when you were small, you always looked ready to walk onto a stage."

She'd been a cute little girl. A beautiful young woman. Dressed to the hilt. Always smiling. Mitch remembered wondering if her folks ever noticed her perfect smile never reached her eyes.

"Pageant life." Anna scrunched up her face. "My mother was so worried I'd scrape a knee or get a bruise that she hated to let me play. By the time I got up the nerve to tell her no more competitions, I was sick of smiling and dressing up."

Mitch cast a sideways glance as they began to swing. "Yet you still always look nice."

"I dress up now because I genuinely like clothes and fashion." Anna pumped her legs and her swing soared high. "I smile because I want to, not to impress some sour-faced judge."

They swung in silence for several seconds. Mitch realized she'd said more to him about her childhood and her feelings than she had the entire summer they were together. He wanted to reciprocate, to tell her what it was like living with a father who didn't know whether you smiled or not because he was too focused on getting to the bottom of a bottle.

The desire to bond with Anna made him keep his mouth shut. The yearning to further this moment of closeness made him keep his mouth shut. And the hope that they could have a meaningful relationship made him keep his mouth shut.

"I don't understand why you think dating will help," Anna said when the silence lengthened.

"When you think of that summer, what do you remember?"

"The thrill. The excitement." Anna's lips curved upward. "Each time we came together was an adventure."

"That's how I recall it, too." His gaze settled on the large golden orb suspended in the sky. "Remember when we snuck to the top of the Hattan building and made love under the full moon?"

"I'll never forget that night." She laughed, a light silvery sound. "Ed Hattan decided to stop by the office. When I heard him on the floor below, I thought we were goners for sure."

"Your heart was beating a thousand beats a minute," Mitch said almost to himself.

"It felt like it was going to jump out of my chest."

"You pressed my hand against your skin so I could feel it." An ache of want washed over Mitch at the memory of her soft breast beneath his fingers. "After that, we forgot about Ed. At least I did."

"It was always like that when we were together," Anna said. "As if nothing else in the world existed."

"We had some hot sex, that's for sure." Mitch

dragged the toe of his boot in the sand and when his swing came to a complete halt, he stood. "But you didn't know what made me tick and I certainly never knew what drove you."

"All these years we've been left to wonder what might have been," Anna mused as her swing slowed to a stop. "Wondering if great sex would have led to a great relationship if given the chance."

Mitch grabbed her hand and tugged her to her feet. "That's why we should date. By the time it ends, there won't be any more unanswered questions."

It felt so natural when Anna wrapped her arms around his neck and slid her fingers through his hair. "How long do you think it will take for us to get sick of each other?"

"I don't know," Mitch said honestly, unable to pull his gaze from her lips. "I guess that's what we're going to find out."

Mitch's mouth lowered to cover hers. The thought of turning away didn't even cross Anna's mind. Her heart pounded against her ribs and blood flowed through her veins like warm honey. When he pulled his sweet lips away after only a handful of seconds, she murmured a protest.

Mitch took a step back and the regret on his face told her that it hadn't been an easy step for him to take.

"Anna." Her name sounded like a caress. With a heart-tugging gentleness, he brushed his knuckles against her cheek. "If this is going to work, we must do it right."

If this is going to work...

Anna's heart gave a little leap but when she spoke, her tone was calm, composed. "Do it right?"

"We need to follow a normal dating protocol," he said plainly.

Anna wasn't sure what *normal protocol* was, but something told her it meant no more kisses tonight. She resisted an urge to sigh. "Give me the bottom line."

He grinned unexpectedly, apparently amused by her sulkish tone. "We should get better acquainted. Do you realize I don't know your favorite color or even what flower you like best?"

Favorite color? Flower? Anna searched his face, looking for any sign he might be kidding, but found none. "Blue is my favorite color."

"Why do you like it?" Mitch asked, sounding truly interested.

"It's the color of the Montana sky." Anna glanced up at the now dark heavens splattered with a million twinkling lights. "No matter where I've lived, seeing a vivid patch of blue overhead always reminds me of home."

"There are blue skies everywhere," Mitch reminded her.

"Not like here."

"Sounds as if you like Montana," he said with a trace of wonder in his tone. "Yet you went away to college and didn't come back."

"I'm back now," she reminded him.

"Temporarily."

"True." Anna glanced up and realized with a start

that they'd left the park behind and were almost to her house.

Mitch slanted a questioning glance in her direction. "Would you consider living here again?"

Anna thought for a moment then shook her head, surprised she'd even entertained the thought. "My dreams aren't here any longer."

Why did that suddenly seem so sad to her?

"Tell me about them," Mitch urged. "Tell me what excites Anna Anderssen."

There was sincerity in his eyes and real interest on his face. It would be easy to answer his question without saying much at all. Yet, she wanted him to know her, to trust her again.

Taking a deep breath, Anna began talking. After a few steps, he took her hand and they strolled down the leaf-strewn sidewalk with the smell of burning wood from neighborhood fireplaces teasing their nostrils. In a voice that occasionally quivered with pent-up emotion, Anna shared her long-held dream of becoming an entrepreneur, of one day owning a boutique.

He listened intently, occasionally stopping to ask her a question. She told him about the classes she'd taken at the University of Denver, the jobs she'd held that had honed her customer-service skills and the talent she'd discovered she possessed for fashion design.

Mitch seemed so interested that when they reached her home, he asked if he could come in and see her sketches.

"I'd love to show them to you." Anna felt herself

flush with pleasure. She climbed the porch steps and he held the screen door open while she rummaged through her purse for the house key.

"Just remember." Anna slid the recalcitrant key into the lock. "Once I show them to you, it'll be my turn to ask you some questions."

A noncommittal smile was his only response.

Anna got him settled on the sofa with a beer and a bowl of chips then hurried up the stairs for her sketches.

When she reached her bedroom on the second floor, she caught a glimpse of herself in the dresser mirror. Bright pink cheeks. Sparkling eyes. A smile she couldn't keep from her lips. This "date" was going better than she'd anticipated. In fact, she couldn't remember the last time she'd had so much fun.

It didn't matter that this was only temporary. Being with Mitch was a very welcome break from the limbo she'd experienced since returning to Sweet River.

Anna ran a brush through her hair, added some color to her lips and then grabbed her portfolio. Eventually this would end but for now, she was determined to enjoy the ride.

Anna stared out the truck window, awed by the colorful foliage that suddenly seemed new. To think she'd almost missed this beauty. When Mitch had called this morning and asked if she wanted to run errands with him, her first impulse had been to say no.

After all, they'd just spent the previous evening together and it had been difficult to keep her hands to herself. She wasn't sure she was strong enough to resist temptation again so soon. Time was what she needed. Time to build up her resistance to him. But before the refusal made it past her lips, Anna remembered a very real purpose behind the invitation.

In order to get sick of each other, they needed to spend time together. That couldn't happen if she stayed home. And since this was her day off, she had the entire day free.

That was why she was in a Dodge 4x4 on this beautiful fall day, headed toward the base of the Crazy Mountains to check the progress of Mitch's new house.

"What made you decide to build out here?" Anna asked when he pulled into a long drive.

"I wanted the privacy," Mitch said, one hand resting lightly on the top of the steering wheel. "Yet something not too far from town."

Anna gazed over the flat pastureland that seemed to go on forever. "It's beautiful country."

A slight smile lifted his lips. "When I was a kid, I never imagined that one day I'd own something like this."

"I'm not surprised," Anna said. "You were always ambitious. I can remember you working at the dude ranch when you were still a boy."

"Henry hired me to exercise his horses." A distant look came over Mitch's face. "I was thirteen. Not old enough to legally work but it was right after my mom died and it gave me something to do."

The flash of sadness in Mitch's beautiful blue eyes tugged at Anna's heartstrings.

"I always liked your mom," she said in a soft voice, realizing this was the first time he'd spoken of his mother and her untimely death. "I don't know if you remember, but she was my Sunday-school teacher the year she passed away. She was so vibrant. So full of life."

A muscle in Mitch's jaw jumped.

"I'm so sorry she died." Anna placed a hand on his arm.

"She'd had stomach pains for days but my dad didn't want her going to the doctor because of the cost." There was no emotion in his voice. Anna could almost believe he was describing the passing of a stranger until she saw the pain in his eyes. "Her appendix burst. We got her to the hospital but there were complications. Everything that could go wrong did."

"I can't imagine."

"Not long after that my dad's drinking got out of control." Mitch's fingers tightened around the steering wheel. "Before Mom died, he'd have a beer or two in the evening. But after she was gone, the alcohol was the only thing that mattered to him."

"He still had you."

"He didn't care about me even before Mom died," Mitch said in an emotionless tone. "Always said I was more trouble than I was worth."

Anna's anger flared. She was seriously tempted to tell Mitch exactly what she thought of such a man. But she swallowed the words, sensing he needed to talk.

"If Henry hadn't given me that job, I don't know how I'd have survived."

She waited for him to continue but he turned silent, almost brooding.

Anna forced a conversational tone. "Did you use the money you earned for college?"

"College?" Mitch's bark of a laugh made her jump. "I used it for food and to pay the utilities."

"But your dad—"

"Drank away his paycheck. I used to have to steal cash from his wallet right after he got paid so we'd have money for rent." Mitch's gaze remained focused on the road.

Shame washed over Anna. While she'd been worrying about which of three dresses to wear to prom, Mitch had been worried about real-life issues. Like his next meal. And keeping warm. "I had no idea."

"It wasn't something I broadcasted. But Seth knew." Mitch's smile didn't reach his eyes. "That's why he invited me to eat at your house so often. Henry and Marg helped out quite a bit, too."

"Why didn't you say something to the sheriff? Or to the school counselor?" Anger at his father, at the life Mitch had been forced to live, rose inside Anna and spilled into her voice. "Someone should have helped you."

"The authorities would only have yanked me out of the house and put me into foster care." Mitch pulled the truck to a stop and flicked off the ignition. "I'd probably have been worse off."

Before she could respond, Mitch shifted his attention to the large home in front of them and his expression turned proud.

"Wow." When he'd said he was building a log home, she'd expected a cabin like the one her family used to have at Pelican Lake. But this elegant house with full-window views, covered porches and stone chimney was no cabin. "It's gorgeous...and humongous."

"There's about five thousand square feet on the main floor." Mitch spoke casually but she could tell her enthusiasm pleased him. "I designed it myself."

"I love all the porches." Anna pushed open the passenger door and hopped out, eager for a closer look. While she waited for him to get out, she surveyed the property, hands on hips. "If Grandma Borghild were here, she'd say all you need is a big patch of prairie coneflowers to have yourself a home."

Mitch tilted his head and she could see his puzzlement.

"Mexican Hats," Anna explained, using the more familiar term. "They were my grandmother's favorite flowers. I love 'em, too."

"I'm going to do basic landscaping but I'll let my wife take care of the flowers," Mitch said.

"Wife?" Anna said in a faint voice that seemed to come from far away. "You plan to marry?"

"Eventually." Mitch smiled and his eyes crinkled. "Once I can quit comparing every woman to you."

Her laughter sounded hollow even to her own ears. He wouldn't stay single for long. Odds were that by the time she left Sweet River, he'd already have someone special at his side. "You want kids?"

"Hell, yes. I want a big family." The words were

confident but the tips of his ears reddened as if he was confessing something horrible. "I never liked being an only child. When I was younger my parents tried but they weren't able to have any more children."

Poor Mitch. He'd had it rough. But one thing stuck out in her mind.

He liked children.

He wanted children.

Lots of children.

Anna's heart sank. Though the breeze held a distinct chill, a trickle of sweat slid down her spine.

"What about you?" he asked. "Do you want a big family?"

Anna's lips froze in a smile. "Maybe."

"You're good with kids," Mitch said unexpectedly. "I know you'll make a great mom."

"How could you possibly know that?" Her tone was sharper than she'd intended and his eyes widened in surprise.

"I've watched you with Seth's little girl," he said, keeping his tone level.

Anna's anger disappeared as quickly as it had appeared.

"I used to think I'd be a good mom," she said, almost to herself. "But that was a long time ago."

Chapter Ten

Mitch moved to stand close to Anna, wondering about the lost look in her eyes. But the construction crew milling around made it neither the time nor the place to exchange confidences. Instead, he followed her lead and refocused on the house.

He couldn't still the pride welling up inside him. He'd come such a long way from his humble beginnings. Finally he would have what he'd longed for all those years ago. "This will be my first home."

Just saying the words made it feel real. He may have purchased the land, drawn up the plans and hired a contractor. He may have helped pour the foundation. But only now, with the windows glimmering in the sun and the house starting to look like a home, did it sink in that his dream was in sight. It felt right. Just like having Anna by his side. That felt right, too.

"Your first home?" Anna slanted a sideways glance at Mitch. "Didn't you have a house in Chicago?"

He lifted a shoulder. "I owned a town house. This feels different. More permanent."

"I know what you mean." Anna nodded in agreement. "Stacie, Lauren and I had a condo in Denver. Of course, we only rented, but even if we had owned it, the place didn't have that forever-after kind of feel."

Mitch was amazed. In a few short sentences Anna had managed to articulate his feelings. All his life he'd longed for the permanence he'd missed as a child. He wanted not just a place to hang his hat but one that would be there year after year. He wanted a woman like that, too. One who would be his best friend. One he could trust with his innermost thoughts and feelings. One to grow old with…and love forever.

Dear God, where had that mushy sentimentality come from? Mitch chuckled and took Anna's arm. "See the guy by the sawhorse? That's Jake Rossie, the job foreman. Let's see if we can get an update."

Confident he'd eventually end up back in Sweet River, Mitch had purchased the land they stood on from Henry three years ago. Last winter the clock had started ticking. He'd given himself twelve months to make the move. In May, he'd returned to Sweet River to kick off the construction of his new home. And this past summer, he'd spent several long weekends in Sweet

The Silhouette Reader Service—Here's how it works: Accepting your 2 free books and 2 free mystery gifts places you under no obligation to buy anything. You may keep the books and gifts and return the shipping statement marked "cancel". If you do not cancel, about a month later we'll send you 6 additional books and bill you just $4.24 each in the U.S. or $4.99 each in Canada. That's a savings of 15% off the cover price. It's quite a bargain! Shipping and handling is just 50¢ per book.* You may cancel at any time, but if you choose to continue, every month we'll send you 6 more books, which you may either purchase at the discount price or return to us and cancel your subscription.

* Terms and prices subject to change without notice. Prices do not include applicable taxes. Sales tax applicable in N.Y. Canadian residents will be charged applicable provincial taxes and GST. Offer not valid in Quebec. All orders subject to approval. Books received may not be as shown. Credit or debit balances in a customer's account(s) may be offset by any other outstanding balance owed by or to the customer. Please allow 4 to 6 weeks for delivery. Offer available while quantities last.

▶ If offer card is missing write to: Silhouette Reader Service, P.O. Box 1867, Buffalo, NY 14240-1867 or visit: www.ReaderService.com ▶

NO POSTAGE
NECESSARY
IF MAILED
IN THE
UNITED STATES

BUSINESS REPLY MAIL
FIRST-CLASS MAIL   PERMIT NO. 717   BUFFALO, NY

POSTAGE WILL BE PAID BY ADDRESSEE

SILHOUETTE READER SERVICE
PO BOX 1867
BUFFALO NY 14240-9952

Send For
2 FREE BOOKS
Today!

I accept your offer!

Please send me two free *Silhouette Special Edition*® novels and two mystery gifts (gifts are worth about $10). I understand that these books are completely free—even the shipping and handling will be paid—and I am under no obligation to purchase anything, ever, as explained on the back of this card.

335 SDL EYMF   **235 SDL EYR3**

Please Print

FIRST NAME

LAST NAME

ADDRESS

APT.#   CITY

STATE/PROV.   ZIP/POSTAL CODE

Visit us online at
www.ReaderService.com

Offer limited to one per household and not valid to current subscribers of *Silhouette Special Edition*® books.

Your Privacy —Silhouette Books is committed to protecting your privacy. Our Privacy Policy is available online at www.eHarlequin.com or upon request from the Silhouette Reader Service. From time to time we make our list of customers available to reputable third parties who may have a product or service of interest to you. If you would prefer for us not to share your name and address, please check here ☐.

▲ Detach card and mail today. No stamp needed. ▲

S-SE-07/09

River checking the progress. Each time he'd been impressed by Jake and his crew.

After listening to Jake this time, Mitch realized the news was better than he'd anticipated. If the weather continued to hold, he should be in his new house before Thanksgiving.

When Jake excused himself to take a phone call, Mitch and Anna headed inside to check out the main level.

Though Anna wasn't nearly as talkative as she'd been on the drive out, she oohed and aahed over everything from the massive wood-burning fireplace to the state-of-the-art kitchen with all the latest appliances.

Upstairs, she admired the large rooms, walk-in closets and open floor plan.

"Tell me what you don't like," he urged.

"Nothing," she said without hesitation. "This is one cool house. If I were you I wouldn't change a thing."

Anna's words pleased him and he found himself explaining his design process. Her questions showed good insight. When the conversation shifted to furniture and interior design possibilities, the discussion turned spirited. They headed to the stairs and Mitch realized how good it felt to have a woman at his side.

Or maybe it only feels good because that woman is Anna.

He dismissed the thought. Of course he was having fun. Everyone knew relationships were always better at the beginning.

"What time is it?" Anna asked.

Mitch glanced at his watch. "Almost noon. Getting hungry?"

She shrugged. "A little."

"I was going to stop at Millstead's," Mitch said. "But we can go back to town now. I can see Henry later tonight."

"I'm not *that* hungry." Anna paused at the bottom of the steps. "Besides, I'd like to say hello to Henry and Marg."

Mitch could barely conceal his surprise. She really *was* a good sport. How had he managed to forget that fact?

Sure, she'd refused to be seen in public with him back then, but she'd willingly—and usually eagerly— gone along with many of his crazy plans. That was why spending time with her had not only been fun but exciting, as well.

Right now the former beauty queen had sawdust on her cheek, hair upended by the wind and jeans that had picked up a nasty streak of dirt during the tour. Still, she'd never looked lovelier.

Mitch fought an almost overwhelming desire to pull her into his arms and make passionate love to her. But he knew such intimacy would only muddy things between them. He clenched his teeth and regained control of his rioting hormones. He might be thirty-three but when it came to Anna, he still had a lot of teenage boy in him.

This intense physical attraction between them had been a major part of what had gone wrong with their previous relationship. They hadn't taken the time to get to know each other. That was a mistake he wouldn't repeat.

Still, what would be the harm with one little touch? He leaned close and brushed golden wood particles from her cheek with the tips of his fingers.

She froze. Her eyes turned dark.

"Sawdust," he said in explanation.

Her gaze remained riveted on his face.

Her tongue moistened her lips.

His body tightened.

Time, he told himself. *Take the time.*

"We'd better get out of here." Mitch crossed the living room. He didn't take a breath until he reached the front door. "I told Henry I'd be there around noon."

"If you want me to hurry, just say so." Smiling, Anna sauntered past him and out the door. He couldn't help noticing how well she filled out her jeans. And he wasn't the only one.

Two carpenters sitting on buckets in the yard eating their lunch stopped chewing to stare at her.

"Sounds like you and Henry are pretty good friends," Anna said.

In fact, the looks on the faces of the construction workers reminded Mitch of men who hadn't eaten in weeks…seeing a juicy T-bone. He shot them a hard look and experienced a surge of satisfaction when they looked away.

"You are, aren't you?" Anna asked.

"Huh?"

"Good friends with Henry?" The dirt crunched beneath her heeled boots as she walked across the yard to the truck.

"I admire him immensely." Mitch paused. "He's been a terrific mentor. There's no one I respect more than Henry Millstead."

In many ways, Henry had been more of a father to him than his own. He'd supported, encouraged and even kicked butt when Mitch had strayed off course.

"It's good you had that influence growing up." Anna climbed into the truck with Mitch's assistance. "If you hadn't, who knows how you might have turned out."

Mitch wished he could say that he'd have ended up just fine, but, remembering some of his teenage escapades, he wasn't so sure. He rounded the truck and hopped inside.

"You may be right," he said once he was behind the wheel. Mitch shifted the truck into gear and pulled out of the yard. "Henry got on my case more times than I can remember. Probably did keep me on the straight and narrow."

One incident in particular stood out in Mitch's memory. After a Friday-night argument with his dad, Mitch had gone drinking with some older friends. He'd overslept and when he'd arrived late for work, Henry had called him into the office. The older man hadn't been heavy-handed or threatening. He hadn't even raised his voice. They'd just talked. Man-to-man. Henry had asked Mitch what he wanted out of life. And then he'd actually listened to the answer.

It had been a life-altering experience. Until that moment, no one had ever bothered to ask him about his hopes and dreams.

For the first time Mitch realized *he* was in control of his future and it was okay to aim high. More important, he'd realized that he wanted more out of life than a hand-to-mouth existence with "Bud" as his best friend.

"The Millsteads were at your high school graduation," Anna remarked. "I know because my parents and I sat next to them.

"I looked for your dad but never did see him," Anna added when the silence lengthened.

"He wasn't there." Though time had eased the pain, the fact that Del—Mitch had started thinking of him as Del that night—hadn't cared to attend his only son's graduation had stung. "He went fishing."

"I can't believe your *father*—" Anna spat the word "—couldn't have picked another day to go fishing."

Her vehemence took Mitch by surprise. "It doesn't matter."

"Of course it does…did." Anna's eyes flashed blue fire. "It was a horrible, nasty, rotten, selfish thing to do."

Mitch smiled. "Tell me how you really feel."

Despite his teasing tone, deep down her anger warmed his heart. She was right. He'd been hurt. Angry. And, okay, maybe a little sad. He hadn't understood why his dad hadn't cared enough to delay his fishing trip. He still didn't understand.

When he'd first heard his dad wasn't going to be

there, he'd decided to skip the commencement activities altogether. Until Henry mentioned how much he was looking forward to seeing his number-one employee walk across the stage.

It had ended up being a very special night. That evening Mitch had learned he was the recipient of a four-year, all-expenses-paid scholarship to college. The scholarship had changed his life.

"I think not showing up was my father's way of preparing me," Mitch said in a philosophical tone.

Anna turned in the seat. "Prepare you for what?"

"He left a week later." Mitch slowed the truck and pulled onto the highway. "That time he didn't come back."

There had been a note. One that made it clear Del didn't intend to return to Sweet River. According to the letter Mitch was now out of high school, therefore an adult in the eyes of the world. Del's obligation was done.

Initially Mitch had been bitter. He'd convinced himself he didn't need anyone. He'd been determined to go it alone and leave Sweet River far behind him. But after two years away he'd realized that he not only missed his friends, he missed Henry and Marg. And Sweet River.

The summer he'd hooked up with Anna had been the first time he'd been "home" since high school. Henry and Marg had opened their home to him. Their warm welcome had brought tears to his eyes. That was when he'd decided that Sweet River would always be home.

And he'd promised himself that one day he'd return for good.

Anna's rejection had smarted but he'd survived. But Mitch didn't want to just survive anymore. He wanted to live life to the fullest.

He'd meant it when he said he wanted a wife and children. That was why he had to get Anna out of his system. Until he did, his heart would never be free.

The Millstead spread sat in a valley, not too far from where Mitch would be making his home.

Mitch slowed the truck as he rounded the last curve in the long drive and the house came into view. He let his gaze linger.

The large white two-story with the wraparound porch and decorative cornices could be on the cover of Home Beautiful. On both sides of the magnificent home were bunkhouses where dude ranch guests stayed who wanted to "rough it." Those who wanted the western experience with a little pampering stayed in the main house, which functioned as a bed-and-breakfast.

A hundred yards to the south stood a picturesque horse barn and corral.

"Wow. It's every bit as lovely as I remembered it." Anna leaned forward and rested her arms on the dash. "I can see why you liked working here. It's such a great atmosphere."

Mitch smiled. How could he make her understand that it was more than that? Every time he turned the bend and saw the house, it was as if he was coming home. The best years of his youth had been spent on this land. The most pleasant memories of his childhood were here.

"What I can't figure out is how you got to and from work," Anna mused. "It's a good ten miles from town. And at thirteen you wouldn't have been old enough to drive."

"One of the ranch hands would pick me up," Mitch said. "When I finished exercising the horses, someone would take me home. That went on until I could drive myself."

"Seems like a lot of work." Anna glanced at him. "I mean, wouldn't it have been easier for Henry to have one of his ranch hands exercise the horses?"

"You make a good point." Mitch realized he'd never given the matter any thought. "Henry always made such a big deal about how much I was helping. I never stopped to think how much work it was for him."

"I'm sure he enjoyed having a child around again," Anna said in a reassuring tone. "His girls were grown and gone. It was just him and Marg."

"It's strange to think of Henry being married to anyone else." Everyone in town knew the story. How Henry's first wife had died of cancer when their children were still in grade school. How lonely he'd been until Marg had moved to Sweet River a couple years later. How Marg hadn't been able to have children but loved his two girls as if they were her own.

"Look. There they are." Anna waved at the couple now standing on the porch.

"They must have heard the truck." Mitch lifted a hand in greeting before parking the truck in a graveled area just east of the barn. Leaving the keys dangling in the ignition, he hopped out and rounded the front to open Anna's door.

As had become his habit, he offered her his hand. For a moment she hesitated before placing her small hand in his and stepping from the vehicle. Her hesitation confused him. Was she apprehensive about seeing Henry and Marg? He'd noticed her touching up her makeup before they arrived. Or was she hesitant about letting Henry and Marg know they were dating? His heart pinged at the thought.

"Are you sure it's okay that I came with you?" Anna whispered when they started toward the house.

The tension that had gripped Mitch's shoulders eased. She was nervous, that was all. Not embarrassed to be seen with him. Not wanting to keep their relationship a secret. Just plain and simple...nervous.

He smiled and grabbed her hand. "Trust me. You've got nothing to worry about."

When they reached the steps to the porch, Anna slipped her hand from Mitch's and held it out. But the Millsteads would have none of that. After she'd been thoroughly hugged and effusively welcomed, everyone headed inside.

"You're going to join us for lunch, I hope," Marg said.

"I don't need to eat," Anna began, "I know you weren't expecting—"

"There's more than enough," Henry said, the warmth of his smile reflected in his eyes.

Mitch gave Anna a questioning glance.

"That'd be great," Anna said.

Marg slipped her arm through Anna's as they climbed the steps. "We made a big pot of beef stew for our lunch guests, but there's plenty left. All the biscuits were gobbled up, but I've got more dough. How would you like to keep me company while I put another batch in the oven?"

"I'd love to," Anna said, struck again by the woman's warm friendliness. "But only if you let me set the table."

"Deal." Marg's smile widened. "That'll give the men a chance to talk while you and I catch up. How is your mother doing? Does she like Bonita Bay as much as your father?"

While placing brightly colored red bowls and plates on the tartan-patterned place mats, Anna updated Marg on her parents' adventures in Florida. Sunlight streamed through the delicately tatted window coverings. The smell of simmering beef and spices filled the air.

Anna could see why Mitch liked it here. It felt like home. A comforting warmth settled around her shoulders like a favorite sweater. If she ever married and had children, she wanted her home to feel just like this one.

"Mitch loves my beef stew," Marg said. "I could give you the recipe if you like."

"Thank you," Anna said, wondering if she should

correct the woman's mistaken impression that she and Mitch were a real couple. But the time somehow didn't seem right. And the reason for their being together was too complicated for a brief explanation.

Marg chatted easily, seeming to have no trouble cooking and talking at the same time. While she rolled and cut out the biscuits and Anna filled the water glasses, they caught up on the past thirteen years.

All too quickly the oven timer buzzed, signaling the biscuits were ready to serve.

The older woman reached for a hot pad and opened the oven door. She glanced up at Anna. "Would you mind telling the men we're ready? By the time they wash their hands, the food will be on the table."

"Sure," Anna said.

"Thank you, Anna." Marg smiled before turning her attention back to the fragrant golden-brown biscuits. "They should be in the den. Just down the hall. Last door on the right."

Before she reached the den, Anna stopped in front of a gilded wall mirror and studied herself with a critical eye. Her hair, though a bit windblown, was acceptable. Unfortunately she couldn't say as much for her face. Her nose was shiny again and her lips definitely in need of more color. Thankfully she'd brought her purse with her.

After a quick touch-up Anna continued down the carpeted hall. She heard Mitch's voice as she neared the doorway. She couldn't make out what he was saying, but when she got closer, she heard her name. She stopped short and held her breath.

"It's not like it was back then," Mitch said, his voice earnest.

"You were hurt badly, Mitch." Henry's voice was so low Anna had to strain to hear the words. "I don't want that to happen again."

"Anna and I—we're grown-up now," Mitch said.

Anna sagged against the wall. Mitch had sworn he hadn't told anyone about their affair in high school. The intensity of her reaction, of the anger that spurted through her veins, surprised her.

Why did it matter that Henry knew they'd once dated? That was old news. And though there was no way Henry—or anyone else, for that matter—could find out about the results of that brief affair, fear still slithered up her spine. She felt as if the secret she'd held close these past thirteen years was being pushed to the surface.

The game she and Mitch were playing, she now realized, was a mistake. Though she was sure that eventually Mitch would tire of her or she of him, so far that hadn't happened. The more they were together, the more she liked him.

Instead of finding herself ready to tell him goodbye, she played the "what if" game. What if the connection she felt was real? What if he cared about her as much as she cared about him? What if they were meant for each other?

She stomped on the wishful thoughts. There could

be no happily-ever-after for her and Mitch. He'd made it clear how he felt about children. He'd never forgive her for what she'd done. Never.

Her time with Mitch had, up to now, been a glorious free fall. The trouble was, if you jumped without a parachute, sooner or later you'd hit the ground.

All Anna could hope was that there was still time to stop the fall.

Chapter Eleven

Anna ignored the jarring ring. Instead of picking up the cordless from its base, she lifted the book higher and stared at the same words she'd been trying to read for the last hour.

Lauren rushed in from the other room and skidded to a stop. "The phone is ringing."

Lifting her gaze from the pages, Anna shrugged. "There's nobody I want to talk to."

As abruptly as it had begun ringing, the phone stilled and clicked to voice mail.

"That might have been a client," Lauren said in an exasperated tone.

"It wasn't a client." Anna spoke in as casual a tone

as she could muster. "I recognized the number on the caller ID."

Lauren stared thoughtfully at Anna for a long moment. "It was Mitch, wasn't it?" Without waiting for confirmation, Lauren dropped down on the sofa next to Anna. "You need to talk to him."

Anna's fingers gripped the novel so tightly the tips turned white. "There's nothing to say."

"From all the messages he's been leaving, my guess is there's plenty to say."

"Well, your guess is wrong." Anna lowered the book to her lap. "Just so you know, Mitch is gone. Out of my life. Like he never existed."

Anna knew she was in trouble when she saw the determined gleam in Lauren's eyes.

"Even though you haven't told me what happened on Monday—" Lauren spoke slowly, appearing to choose her words carefully "—something happened. And despite this 'tough girl' facade of yours, I know you're hurting."

There was a softness in Lauren's voice, an understanding in her eyes that reminded Anna that this wasn't just a roommate, this was her good friend. To Anna's horror, several tears slipped down her cheeks. She quickly brushed them away with the tips of her fingers.

Anna swallowed the lump that had somehow lodged in her throat. "It's over between us."

"Did he offend you in some way?" Lauren took Anna's cold hand in hers. "Is that why he's calling? To apologize?"

"He didn't do anything wrong," Anna said. "I just can't do this anymore."

"Can't do what?"

"Date him."

"Why not?"

"It's just—" Anna paused. Over the past two days she'd pulled out her phone more times than she could count, her fingers itching to dial his number, her heart longing to hear his voice. "I have concerns. I don't think we have a shot in hell of being happy long-term."

The two tiny frown lines between Lauren's brows deepened. "Have you discussed these concerns with Mitch?"

"There's nothing to say." Anna's voice started out loud but she reined it in. She wasn't angry with Lauren. Her friend was an honorable, trustworthy woman. No, at the moment the person Anna was most angry with was herself. For believing in the fairy tale. For thinking that if you wanted something hard enough, it—

"Anna?"

Anna looked up and blinked.

"Are you even listening to me?" Lauren asked.

"I'm sorry." Anna refocused on Lauren. "What were you saying?"

"You must talk to him about these concerns of yours." Lauren softened the directive with a sympathetic smile.

Anna laid her book on the side table and heaved a resigned sigh. "Tenacious" could be her friend's middle name. "We dated a couple times. It didn't work out. I don't see any reason to call him back. He's a smart guy. Eventually he'll get the message."

Okay, so it was a juvenile way to handle the situation. Definitely a coward's way out. She could kick herself for not telling him on the way back from the Millstead ranch. But he'd been in such a good mood, and she didn't want to spoil it.

"I've seen you do this far too many times," Lauren said.

Anna lifted a brow.

"Each time you begin to get close to a guy, you get scared and pull away. Or you push him away."

"This is way different." The solid floor beneath Anna's feet turned to quicksand. "With those guys, the spark just wasn't there."

"What about Mitch?" Lauren pinned Anna with her gaze. "Is the spark there?"

"Yes," Anna grudgingly admitted. "But that doesn't matter because—"

"Don't you see," Lauren said as she touched a finger against Anna's lips, "you're sabotaging your own chance at happiness. It's almost as if you don't feel you deserve to be happy."

I don't.

The admission rose unbidden from the deepest recesses of her soul.

"Of course I deserve to be happy," Anna insisted. "But I can't be happy with Mitch."

"Then talk to him," Lauren urged. "Tell him the relationship isn't working for you. If you care at all about him, be honest."

Be honest. It sounded so simple. Did Lauren even realize what she was asking?

Still, there was no doubt in Anna's mind that what her friend suggested was the right thing to do. Without giving herself time to chicken out, Anna picked up the phone and dialed Mitch's cell. He answered on the first ring.

"Hello, Mitch."

"Anna." Even with the static on the line, the relief in his voice came through loud and clear. "I've been trying to reach you for two days."

"Are you at home?"

"I just walked through the door."

"Can I come over?"

"Sure," he said without hesitating. "Is something the matter?"

"We need to talk."

We need to talk.

The words ran round and round in Mitch's head as he showered and pulled on clean clothes.

Anna had been distant on the ride back from Henry's ranch on Monday, but he'd told himself she was tired. The past couple of days he'd been busy getting the con- tractors lined up to begin renovations on The Hattan. He'd called Anna a handful of times, but they hadn't connected.

That there might be something wrong hadn't even crossed his mind. Alex had been back in his office on Tuesday and Mitch knew Anna had worked both yesterday and today. He'd assumed she was busy with work and helping Stacie with last-minute wedding plans. If they hadn't connected tonight, he would have stopped by her house tomorrow.

But something in her tone told him there was more going on than just being busy.

Mitch headed down the stairs. Once he reached the kitchen, he uncorked a bottle of merlot—Anna's favorite—and grabbed two glasses. He'd barely put them on a table in the living room when the doorbell rang. He glanced at his watch. Anna had made the trip in record time.

"What did you do, fly?" he asked, pulling open the door.

But instead of Anna, Cassie stood on the porch. "I hope I'm not intruding."

She moved forward as if to step inside but Mitch kept his hand on the doorjamb, blocking her entry.

"Now's not a good time, Cass." He shook his head. "Anna's on her way over."

Though he'd kept his tone deliberately casual, some of his worry must have seeped through because Cassie's gaze turned sharp and assessing. "Trouble?"

"No trouble," Mitch said easily. "We just haven't seen each other in a couple days. You understand."

"Of course." Cassie smiled and shoved a plate into his hands that he didn't even realize she'd been holding. "I made some pumpkin cookies today for the boys. I thought you might like some, too."

"Thanks." Mitch didn't even glance down at the

cookies. He was too focused on the car pulling up to the curb.

"I'd better go," Cassie said. "Wouldn't want to get you in any trouble."

Mitch started to say there was no chance but stopped when Anna got out of the car. The look on her face and the determined set of her jaw told him he *was* in trouble. Big trouble. And he had the feeling he would soon know why.

Anna started toward the porch where Mitch stood waiting. She ran into Cassie where the driveway met the sidewalk.

"I just dropped off a plate of pumpkin cookies with some yummy cream cheese frosting. Make sure Mitch shares with you."

Two days ago Anna might have been jealous, wondering why Cassie was with Mitch every time she turned around. But right now her thoughts were focused on the handsome cowboy standing on the porch with a welcoming smile on his face. Her heart rose to her throat.

Dear God, give me strength to do what needs to be done.

Straightening her shoulders, Anna said goodbye to Cassie and walked to the porch.

As she drew closer, a look of pure masculine appreciation filled Mitch's gaze.

The realization that she looked her best bolstered Anna's confidence. Before she'd left her house, she'd taken a few minutes to freshen her makeup and hair. She'd also changed into a favorite pair of tweed pants with a form-fitting sweater.

"You look nice this evening," Mitch said.

"Thank you." Anna tried to smile but her lips refused to move into position. "May I come inside for a moment?"

"I thought we could talk out here."

For a second Anna was taken aback. Until she realized this must mean he wanted to keep the conversation brief. Which told her he knew why she was here.

"Okay." The fact that Anna could see Mrs. Barbee at the window was reassuring. At least the woman wasn't skulking around the yard, hiding behind a bush. "I can make this quick."

"I was just teasing. You're not making anything quick." Mitch laughed. "You're coming inside and having a glass of merlot with me."

He moved aside and held the door for her. For a second Anna hesitated. When she heard the Barbees' front door creak open, she stepped inside.

"Have a seat." Mitch gestured to the sofa. "Are you hungry? I could get you something to eat?"

"I won't be here long enough to eat." Anna dropped down into the leather chair.

His smile vanished at her clipped tone. He shut the front door and took a seat on the sofa. Leaning forward, he rested his arms on his thighs, giving her his full attention. "What's on your mind?"

"I don't want to see you anymore."

"What?"

"You heard me."

He sat back. His brows pulled together in a frown. "I assume you have a reason."

"I do." Anna folded her hands in her lap, the slamming of her heart against her ribs at odds with her outwardly cool demeanor.

"I overheard you talking to Henry in the den."

"And?"

"He knew all about us."

Mitch stood and raked a hand through his hair. He took a deep breath. "Henry knows we dated that summer. He doesn't know we slept together."

"You swore you hadn't told anyone." Anna's voice shook with emotion.

"It wasn't easy, you know." Mitch turned toward the front window and gazed into the darkness. "Losing you."

The anguish in his voice tugged at her heartstrings.

"It wasn't easy for me, either," Anna said softly.

Mitch returned to the sofa. "When I left the street dance that night, I went back to Henry's ranch." A muscle in his jaw moved. "That's when one of his hands and I got into it."

"What happened?" Anna told herself none of this mattered, but she couldn't help being curious.

"Henry had come home from the celebration early." Mitch's tone remained even. "He heard the shouting. Came out. Pulled us apart. Sent Cyrus to the bunk-house. Ordered me inside."

"That's when you told him what I'd done." It was a wonder Henry had been so welcoming to her at his own home much less at the soup supper.

"I told him that you and I'd been dating and that we'd broken up." Mitch met her gaze. "That's all I said."

"He doesn't think us dating again is a good idea."

"That came through loud and clear," Mitch said, surprising her with a chuckle.

"He doesn't like me."

"That isn't it at all." Mitch leaned forward and grabbed her hands. "He's worried about me. And about you."

"Why me?"

"Probably because I told him I was to blame when we broke up before."

"Oh my goodness, you weren't to blame. You—"

"Sure I was," Mitch said. "I wasn't good at expressing my feelings. I'm still not great at it. That's why you felt so insecure back then. That's why you did what you did."

The tightness in Anna's chest began to ease. "You should tell him what we're doing now. How we're—"

"Absolutely not." Mitch's fingers tightened around hers. "That's between you and me. No one else."

This was the time for her to tell him the game was over. But as his thumbs began to massage the tops of her hands, her carefully prepared speech disappeared in a flood of emotion. She wasn't sure how it happened, but the tension between them had been replaced by pleasurable warmth.

"I don't want there to be any secrets between us," Mitch said.

"Neither do I," Anna said between suddenly dry lips.

"I'm really enjoying spending time with you." His expectant gaze met hers.

"It has been fun."

"Come over here." He tugged on her hands and gestured with his head toward the spot on the sofa next to him.

Tell him now, a tiny voice of reason in her head urged, *tell him about the baby.* She ignored the voice and settled down next to Mitch instead.

He slipped an arm around her shoulder and pulled her to him.

"Are we okay?" he asked in a low voice.

Anna leaned her head against him. "We're okay."

He expelled a breath she didn't even realize he'd been holding. "Good."

"Good indeed," Anna murmured.

"Thank you for coming to talk to me," Mitch said. "For giving me a chance to explain."

Her gaze fused with his. She'd had a chance to step back to safety but instead had chosen to jump. She lifted her face and wrapped her arms around his neck. The free fall had begun.

Chapter Twelve

"Surely there's something I can do to help." Anna leaned over Stacie's shoulder, filched a piece of broccoli from the salad her friend was mixing and then popped it into her mouth. "Mmm, this is good."

Stacie gave Anna's hand a little slap. "You want to help? Keep your fingers out of the salad."

There was no rancor in her friend's voice, only good-natured teasing. After all, it was too beautiful a day for any negative emotion. The sun shone through the windows in Anna's kitchen. Outside, under brilli-ant blue skies, hamburger patties and chicken breasts cooked slowly over charcoal.

If the calendar hadn't said it was mid-October, Anna would have thought it was summertime. When she and her friends had planned this Friday-night get-together last month, Anna had thought they'd be eating warm comfort food in front of the fireplace. She'd also planned it would be just the three women and Josh. But with his daughter, Dani, attending a church event, Seth had been at loose ends. When Josh had invited Seth, Anna saw no choice but to invite Mitch.

No choice.

Anna chuckled. Who was she kidding? She'd been eager to see him again. He was here now, just outside, flipping burgers and drinking beer with Seth and Josh while Anna and her friends finished up the side dishes.

At the table, Lauren was topping chocolate cupcakes with thick buttercream frosting. Anna had just finished cutting up apples and blending them into a Waldorf salad.

"I'm done." Lauren stepped back from the table and admired her work. "I did a pretty good job, if I do say so myself."

Anna glanced at the little cakes with the perfectly swirled icing, now artfully arranged on a crystal platter. "Lovely and definitely de-lish."

"I'm finished, too," Stacie announced. "Once the hamburgers and chicken are done, we should be ready to eat."

"Hallelujah." Josh strolled into the kitchen and slipped an arm around his fiancée's waist. He glanced down and a slow grin stole over his face. "Broccoli salad is one of my favorites."

The declaration had barely left his lips when he plucked a floret from the top of the salad.

"Joshua Collins." Stacie wagged a finger at the cowboy. "You're as bad as Anna."

"Who's as bad as Anna?" Mitch asked, his gaze seeking her out the moment he stepped into the kitchen.

"No one." Anna felt her knees turn to putty at the smoldering look Mitch gave her. "I'm the ultimate bad girl."

"What did you do this time?" Mitch asked, playing along.

"Stole one teeny-weeny piece of broccoli from the salad," Anna admitted. "And had one of Lauren's cupcakes as an appetizer."

"Stacie's right, man." Josh turned to Mitch, his expression serious. "You've got yourself a bad one."

The room erupted in laughter. Anna wondered if she was the only one who caught the significance of Josh's words. She and Mitch were now seen as a couple. Until they got sick of each other and the game came to an end. Or until he found out about...

"Hey." Mitch's voice was soft and low. She looked up and found him at her side. "Don't let what Josh said bother you."

Anna glanced around but the others were all laughing and talking as they carried the food outside.

"You and I know the score," he continued. "That's what matters."

At first she didn't understand. Then it hit her. He thought she was upset because Josh had labeled them a couple.

"I thought it was sweet." Anna turned and looped her arms around his neck. "After all, you are my boyfriend."

He smiled and settled his hands on her hips. "Until you get sick of me."

She slid her fingers through his soft wavy hair. "Or until you get sick of me."

His blue eyes met hers and warmed her all over. Talking on the phone several times yesterday had been nice but nothing beat the personal…touch.

"I'm not sick of you yet." He pulled her hips forward until their bodies fit together perfectly.

She tightened her hold around his neck, drawing his face closer to hers. "I'm not sick of you, either."

His head lowered and she breathed in the delicious scent of his cologne. When his lips touched hers, the fluttering in her belly turned to an ache.

Apparently not feeling the same sense of urgency, Mitch took his time. He sipped rather than gulped, his lips teasing, not demanding.

After a couple of attempts to get him to rush from zero to steamy, Anna gave in to the moment and enjoyed the closeness. But when his tongue brushed her lips and she opened her mouth to him, the urgency returned. Warmth gave way to heat.

Though there didn't seem to be any space between them, Anna pressed herself even closer. A shiver of desire danced up her spine at the feel of his hard length against her belly.

His hands slid up her sides until his thumbs rested just below her breasts. Fire torched her veins and Anna heard herself moan, a low sound of want and need….

"Stacie wondered if you could bring out—" Seth

stopped and grinned. "Can't you two keep your hands to yourselves?"

Anna jerked back from Mitch's arms, resisting the urge to smooth her hair and straighten her sweater.

"What does Stacie need?" To Anna's horror, her voice came out an octave higher than normal.

"Some ketchup and mustard." Seth's smile widened a notch. "Since you two are…busy, I'll take them to her."

Heat flooded Anna's cheeks, but she told herself she wasn't embarrassed. And there certainly wasn't any reason to apologize.

"Is it time to eat?" Mitch looked surprisingly unruffled and irritatingly self-composed.

Seth opened the refrigerator and grabbed the condiments. "Once these are on the table, it will be."

Mitch's arm slipped around Anna's shoulders as naturally as if he'd been doing it for years instead of a few weeks. "We'll be right out."

Seth chuckled. "No rush."

Once they were alone again, Anna lifted her face to Mitch. "Saved by the brother."

Mitch's brow hitched up.

"Give us another five minutes and we'd have been rolling around on the floor." Her heart picked up speed at the erotic image.

"Too cold." Mitch shook his head. "I had my eye on that wall over there."

Anna's mouth went dry.

"Don't tell me you forgot how much fun we had in

the utility closet of the civic center," Mitch said when the silence lengthened.

"I remember." Anna's heart did a double backflip in her chest. "It was at Andrea Barbee's wedding dance."

His eyes turned dark. "You were with your friends. I was with mine."

"We hadn't been together in days—"

"I wanted you so much—" he began.

"There was only enough room in the closet to stand."

Mitch winked. "Where there's a will, there's a way."

Her breathing grew shallow. He'd taken her against the door, his mouth swallowing her cries of pleasure. Only later had Anna realized they hadn't used a condom.

"I've never forgotten that night," he added.

Anna forced a light tone past her tight lips. "Neither have I."

The repercussions of that encounter still haunted her dreams. Why hadn't she called a halt when she realized he didn't have a condom? He'd tried to stop but she'd kissed him hard and assured him it was an okay time of the month.

She'd learned a harsh lesson that night. As in horse racing, long shots sometimes do come in.

Mitch trailed a finger down her cheek. "We'll have to try it again. See if that position was really as good as we remember."

Anna leaned into his caress. While she knew that being intimate again made no sense, tonight had proven what she'd known all along.

The electrical charge, the pull that had existed between the two of them all those years ago still snapped and popped. In fact, the energy was stronger than ever. While she'd do her part to keep the physical stuff at bay, one of these days she'd end up in his bed. It was inevitable.

Anna could only hope that when that happened, she would be strong enough to keep her heart out of the equation. Because, given time, this would all come to an end. And she'd need to be able to move on.

Chapter Thirteen

Thunder Lanes, Big Timber's newest bowling alley, buzzed with excitement. Rock music filled the air and brightly colored lights strobed the lanes. In less than fifteen minutes, moonlight bowling would begin.

Mitch finished lacing up his shoes then turned to check on Anna's progress. His lips curved in a smile as he watched her lift one ball after another, her brow furrowed in concentration.

After the barbecue earlier in the evening, each couple had gone their separate ways. Josh and Stacie had left for his ranch to practice their "vows." The look in his friend's eye when he gazed at his pretty fiancée told Mitch that vows weren't the only thing the two lovebirds would be practicing.

Seth had left shortly after when the church had called. The event Dani was attending had gotten out early. Lauren had volunteered to ride with Seth to pick up his daughter.

That left Mitch and Anna alone. After the kiss in the kitchen, Mitch knew exactly how he'd like to spend the rest of the evening. That was why he'd suggested moonlight bowling. He couldn't imagine a less romantic setting than a noisy bowling alley.

"I've found it," Anna said, a note of triumph in her voice. "The perfect ball for me."

A red, black and gray Brunswick ball dropped into the rack next to his with a thud. Anna turned around, her eyes snapping with anticipation. "Can we start now?"

When Anna had told him she'd never bowled, he'd almost suggested they do something different. Until he'd reminded himself that if they were really dating, they'd be trying new activities and getting a feel for each other's likes and dislikes.

Although she'd insisted on wearing her skirt rather than changing into something more comfortable, she seemed eager to learn the game.

"Any minute," Mitch said. "Once the other couple arrives, we'll start."

"I wish it could have been just you and me." Her smile wavered. "Especially since this is my first time."

"I wish that, too." Mitch had tried to convince Larry, the manager, to let the two of them bowl alone. That was when he was told moonlight bowling was a big night and the owner wanted the place filled to capacity. Since they didn't have another couple with them, they'd get whoever walked in.

Two middle-aged couples were already seated in the same area using the other lane. From the language they were throwing around—Christmas tree, Cincinnati, clothesline—they were obviously experienced bowlers. For Anna's sake, Mitch hoped whatever couple they got wouldn't be very good.

"Here we are. Lane ten." The male voice was familiar. Mitch looked up and nearly groaned aloud.

"Alex." Anna sounded as surprised as he felt. "And Cassie. What are you doing here?"

"This is great." Alex's lips lifted in a broad smile. "When Cassie and I decided to try moonlight bowling we wished there was another couple we could go with…and here you are."

Mitch watched the two take seats next to Anna and unzip their bags. He knew Cassie bowled so he wasn't surprised she'd brought her own bag. But the fact that Alex had one, too, *did* surprise him. "Have you bowled much, Darst?"

"In college." Alex slipped off his loafers and pulled a pair of black and gray bowling shoes from his bag. "I joined a league a couple years ago when the sport experienced a resurgence in popularity."

"What was your average?" Mitch hoped for a low number. After all, just because a guy played on a league didn't necessarily mean he was any good.

"One eighty," Alex said.

The attorney tossed the number out there like it was nothing. But that average meant Alex was clearly no slouch. With both him and Cassie being experienced bowlers, that left Anna as the odd one out. And Mitch knew that wouldn't be a comfortable position for her.

"Is one eighty good?" Anna asked Alex. "This is my first time."

"It's on the low side," Alex said.

"Then I hope I can do that well," Anna said.

Alex and Cassie exchanged an amused look. Mitch's blood began to boil.

"Tonight isn't about competition," Mitch said. "It's about having fun."

There was a warning underlying his light tone that he hoped came through loud and clear. Nobody was going to make Anna feel bad tonight.

Cassie went first and picked up her spare. Alex got a strike. When it was Anna's turn, she shuffled down the approach with such awkwardness that Mitch's heart tightened.

A harsh buzz sounded.

She jumped then spun around, the ball still in her hand. "What was that?"

"It means you fouled." Mitch stood and pointed to the white line at the end of the approach. "If you go over that, you get the buzzer."

"So I need to get rid of the ball before I reach that line, right?" Anna asked.

"Right." Mitch smiled reassuringly. "Do you remember how to aim for the marks?"

Anna nodded before her attention shifted to the pins at the end of the alley. This time her approach was better but she twisted her hand when she released the ball. It headed straight for the gutter, falling in with a loud thud.

Alex chuckled. "Ball in the moat."

Mitch shot him a sharp look.

Two bright spots of color dotted Anna's cheeks. "I've never been very athletic."

"You did fine," Mitch assured her. "If you wouldn't have turned your hand at the last minute, you might have had a strike."

Her eyes brightened. "Really?"

"You bet." Mitch waited until her ball was back in the rack before he stood and handed it to her. "Let me help you."

If she turned down his offer, he'd back off. He'd dated plenty of women who refused to accept any sort of help or advice, no matter how well-meaning.

"How are you going to do that?" Anna asked, more curious than resistant.

"I'll show you." He walked with her until they were just behind the line. "I'm going to put my arm around you and we're going to throw this bad boy together. Okay?"

Anna nodded.

He stood behind her and inhaled her clean, fresh scent. Leaning close, he put his right arm behind hers. "Keep the inside of your wrist toward the pins."

Slowly she pulled her arm back, then jerked it forward and released the ball.

It chugged, chugged, chugged down the lane.

"We got a creeper," Alex called out.

Mitch took a deep breath and bit back a harsh reply. He let his breath out slowly as the ball continued to roll. Finally, after what seemed an eternity, it reached the pins, knocking down three on the right.

"You won." Mitch gave her an exuberant hug. "You've got a six-pack of Pepsi."

Anna's jaw dropped. "By knocking down *three* pins?"

"By knocking down the red pin," Mitch clarified.

"These little incentives only happen during moonlight bowling," Cassie added. "There'll be prizes like that to win all night."

Anna smiled. "I'm beginning to like this game."

Mitch exhaled the breath he didn't realize he'd been holding.

The rest of the evening flew by. Alex appeared more relaxed as the night progressed. He and Cassie spent most of the evening laughing and talking and engaging in some friendly wagering.

Anna didn't even break seventy her first game but she didn't appear to care. And even after she'd seemed to get the hang of the approach and release, she still asked Mitch for pointers.

By the time they'd finished the second game, the bowling alley was closing.

"This has been really fun." Instead of looking at Mitch, Cassie's eyes were on Alex. "We'll have to do it again sometime."

"Definitely." Alex smiled at the pretty brunette.

"Drive safely," Anna called out several minutes later when the other couple walked off, Alex's arm slung around Cassie's shoulders.

Instead of getting up, Anna leaned back in the molded plastic seat. "When I lived in Denver, if anyone had asked me to go bowling I would have laughed in their face."

"Not your kind of activity?" Mitch dropped down beside her and hid his disappointment. He'd thought she'd had a good time.

"I didn't think so." She reached over and took his hand, lacing her fingers through his. "But I had fun tonight. And I'd like to do it again sometime."

"I'm glad you enjoyed yourself." The weight pressing down on Mitch's shoulders eased.

"It just makes me wonder...."

"Wonder what?"

She expelled a breath that could have been a sigh. "How many other opportunities have I let pass me by?"

Mitch tilted his head.

"When Cassie was talking tonight about opening a shop in The Hattan, I found myself feeling envious."

He waited for her to continue.

"She's pursuing her dream while mine is still simmering on the back burner."

"I've got more space." Mitch still wasn't sure where she was going with this. "You could open your boutique."

"Thanks for the offer, but I have to be realistic,"

Anna said with a rueful smile. "Sweet River just isn't large enough to sustain a clothing boutique."

After a moment, Mitch nodded. He couldn't argue with her logic.

"Remember when Cassie talked about how great it would be if her seamstress business could be part of a larger, more eclectic shop?"

Mitch vaguely remembered Cassie mentioning something to that effect somewhere between the first and second game.

"My mind was so closed I hadn't even considered that as an option." Anna gazed off into the distance. "I've done too much of that in my life. Instead of seeing all possibilities, I've kept a narrow focus."

Mitch stilled. Anna had made it clear that when Lauren returned to Denver, she was going with her. Now it appeared she was having second thoughts. He tried, but failed, to stop the excitement rising up inside him. "Are you saying you'd be open to the possibility of staying in Sweet River?"

"I don't know," Anna said slowly. "If you'd asked me a month ago—or even two weeks ago—I'd have said 'absolutely not.'"

"Now?" Mitch asked.

"Now," Anna said as she leaned close and brushed her lips across his, "I'm keeping all my options open."

Chapter Fourteen

Bowling and church. Dating in Sweet River didn't get much better. Two days after her success at Thunder Lanes, Anna tucked herself snugly in the pew next to Mitch. When he'd asked her to go to Sunday services with him, she'd almost said no. Though she'd grown up in the church, over the past thirteen years she'd drifted away. In the crowd she ran with in Denver, faith had not been a priority.

In Sweet River, Sunday services were an integral part of the community. Not only a place to worship, but a place to see and be seen. If Mitch had wanted to test her willingness to be seen in public with him, he'd picked the perfect venue. But Anna had the feeling they'd both moved past such game playing.

The desire to spend time with Mitch had led her to say yes. Yet Lauren's constant preaching about the importance of living a holistic lifestyle had also had an impact. Anna realized she'd been neglecting her spiritual life.

Though she wasn't sure much could be accomplished in a single Sunday, Anna was here to give it a shot. And she couldn't resist a little teasing.

"When I said it was your turn to pick where we would go on our next date, I never expected to be spending the morning with Pastor Barbee," Anna said in a low tone meant for Mitch's ears only.

Even while she was speaking, Anna lifted a hand to return the wave of Norm Kreps, the checker-playing virtuoso from the café.

"This is part of my life." Mitch scooted closer to Anna to make room for a family of three. "I wanted to share it with you."

"I never realized you were a churchgoer."

"When my mom was alive, we came every Sunday." Mitch slipped his arm around her shoulders as two more people slid into the other end of the pew.

Closer than ever to Mitch's side, Anna breathed in the enticing scent of his cologne. Her heart danced a salsa beat against her ribs. The feel of Mitch's hand on her shoulder and the warmth of his thigh against hers brought memories of when they'd been much closer than this.

"My dad didn't see it as important."

Anna blinked. "Didn't see what as important?"

"Church." Mitch's lips rose in a humorless smile. "After being out drinking Saturday nights, sitting in a pew was the last place he wanted to be on Sunday mornings."

"I quit going when I went away to college," Anna admitted.

The notes of the first hymn rang out from the ancient pipe organ and conversation came to a halt. The song was a familiar one and Anna knew the words by heart.

She checked out who was in attendance while she sang. Stacie and Josh sat up front with Lauren while Cassie and her boys were on the other side of the aisle. Henry and Marg Millstead sat close to Anna's brother, Seth, and her niece, Dani, two rows in front of Cassie.

Anna breathed in the atmosphere. This was small-town America at its finest. The air might be brisk outside and storm clouds might hang low in the sky. But inside the white clapboard building with the picturesque steeple, a cohesive community came together in warm fellowship.

When Mitch stepped to the pulpit to read the Bible verse, Anna cast a sideways glance at Henry Millstead. The pride in her heart was reflected on the older gentleman's face.

Mitch looked so handsome in his navy suit and stylish tie, confident and at ease. There was no evidence of the rebellious youth who'd once felt so out of place.

Mitch nodded to his mentor and slipped back into the pew, next to Anna.

It was amazing, she thought, how you could see a man you'd known your whole life in a new way.

When it was time for the sermon, Anna prepared herself for a mental snooze-fest. Though it had been years since she'd heard Pastor Barbee preach, she'd never thought of him as a particularly inspiring speaker. But as the words flowed from the minister's lips, Anna was forced to admit she'd been mistaken. Either he'd improved, or back then she'd been too young to fully appreciate his message. When he told the story of the prodigal son, twisting it to make it relevant to modern day, Anna hung on every word.

Perhaps it was because she could empathize with the younger son. In her own way, she'd been spoiled and pampered. She'd also been eager to strike out on her own. But after more than a decade of taking advantage of everything a large urban center had to offer, she could finally see the trade-offs. Yes, she'd had movies and plays and theater events at her disposal. But the anonymity of the city could feel cold and impersonal at times.

In Sweet River, the social life consisted of ice cream socials, card parties and bowling. And forget anonymity. In a small town, everything was up close and personal.

"How many of us would turn a prodigal son away?" Anna refocused her attention on the sermon.

"How many of us keep needed forgiveness locked in our hearts?"

Beside her, Anna felt Mitch stiffen slightly. She wondered if he was thinking of his dad and all the crummy things Del had done.

But as the pastor continued to talk, Anna found the message touching her own heart. Unlike Mitch, it wasn't her father she had difficulty forgiving, it was her mom.

Anna sighed and glanced at Mich. His jaw was now clenched. Impulsively, Anna slipped her fingers through his, wordlessly offering him comfort.

Even when it came time for the closing prayers, he didn't release her hand. By the time the organ had wheezed the last note of the closing hymn, a sense of peace had stolen over Anna. If the prodigal son could be forgiven by God and his family, there might be a chance for her.

She'd been barely eighteen. Living in a distant city. Far from family and friends. Mitch had made it perfectly clear what he thought of her. But not telling him about the baby had been a mistake.

A familiar ache filled her heart. The fact that she'd handle the situation much differently now didn't lessen her guilt.

Still, the sermon had given her hope.

Perhaps one day she'd confess the whole story and ask Mitch for his forgiveness.

Perhaps one day he'd forgive her.

Perhaps one day she might even be able to forgive herself.

Mitch stood on the porch of the old Victorian and hoped he wasn't overreacting. It was now Wednesday. Since Sunday, he'd seen Anna every day. And when he wasn't with her, he was talking to her on the phone. Long conversations that made him feel like a teenager in the throes of love.

Though he'd known Anna since she was a skinny kid in pigtails, he felt as if he was getting acquainted with her for the first time. And slowly but surely, Mitch found himself falling in love with her all over again.

But this love was different. This wasn't the love of a boy for a pretty girl, but the love of a man for a woman. Though Mitch had sworn he wasn't going to let himself fall for Anna again, now that it had happened he wasn't scared.

He hadn't held anything back. He'd been open and honest with her. She'd been the same. There were no secrets standing between them now.

That was why he found himself standing on her porch at ten thirty in the evening. He'd called and left numerous messages all day. She hadn't called him back, not once.

While he realized she could simply be busy finalizing plans for Stacie's prenuptial dinner tomorrow night, it didn't seem likely. Yesterday, she'd told him everything was in place for tomorrow's festivities.

Maybe he was being paranoid but if she was upset with him, he wanted to know so he could make it right. He wanted her to know, to believe, that there wasn't anything she couldn't bring to him. No issue was big enough that they couldn't work through it together.

Mitch let his knuckles fall on the door in a soft rap. Though a lamp was on in the parlor, the lights were off upstairs. He hated to wake her but he wouldn't be able to sleep until she confirmed all was well between them.

He lifted his hand to knock again when the door opened.

Anna stood in the doorway. But this was an Anna he'd never seen before. Her blond hair was pulled back from her face in what could be called a ponytail, though there was as much hair out of the rubber band as there was in it.

Her eyes were swollen and red-rimmed, her face pale and blotchy. But what surprised him most was her attire—gray sweatpants and a faded, long-sleeved tee. An outfit Anna would normally never consider wearing. Unease crawled up his spine.

She pushed a strand of limp hair back from her face. "It's late."

"I was worried." Mitch brushed past her and stepped inside, not bothering to wait for an invitation.

Though the lamp in the parlor spilled light into the foyer, the rest of the house was quiet and dark. He glanced around. "Where is everyone?"

"Stacie is staying over at Josh's," Anna said in a dull tone. "Lauren had a horrible migraine. She took enough medicine to knock out a bull and went straight to bed."

So far, everything sounded normal. But something was wrong. The puzzle pieces weren't fitting together. Though she hadn't asked him to stay, Mitch shrugged out of his jacket, hung it on the coat rack and turned to face her.

"What's wrong, Anna?" He found himself using the same soft, low tone that kept his Pryor horses from spooking. "And please don't tell me 'nothing,' because I know better."

Anna gestured with her head toward the parlor. "Why don't you have a seat. I'll get us some tea."

"Can I help?"

She shook her head. "It'll just take a sec."

Mitch had barely sat down on the antique sofa when she returned with two steaming cups. He rose to his feet. She handed one cup to him, keeping the other for herself.

Mitch took a sip and waited.

"I'm sorry I didn't call you back." She stared into her cup. "I was superbusy at work. And then, just when I was getting off, I received some distressing news."

"What kind of news?" Mitch gently probed when she didn't continue.

Her fingers tightened around the cup but she remained silent.

"Tell me," Mitch urged.

Anna looked up. "My parents were involved in a serious car accident."

Mitch took a step forward. "Are they okay?"

"Dad was having chest pains. They thought he was having a heart attack. But thankfully his lab and EKG were normal. They decided it was just the stress of the accident." Several tears slipped down Anna's cheeks. "My parents' friends, the other couple who were in the car with them, were killed."

"Oh, Anna, honey." Mitch took the tea from her hand and set both cups aside, then pulled her trembling body into his arms. "What about your mother? Was she hurt?"

"She has a slight concussion and some bumps and bruises, but other than that she's okay. I offered to fly down and help out but she said no. I just keep thinking…"

Her voice faltered and his heart twisted at the lost look in her eyes.

"Keep thinking what?" he probed.

"If they hadn't let their friends drive, if they'd been sitting in the front, they'd be in the morgue right now." The words had barely left her lips when she began to sob.

Although Anna hadn't enjoyed the close relationship with her parents that her brother had, she still loved them. Until she'd gotten the news about the accident, she hadn't realized how much.

After a few minutes of letting the tears fall, she relaxed enough to lay her cheek against Mitch's chest. As he stroked her hair, she listened to the steady beat of his heart and felt comforted.

This was new territory. All her life she'd had to be the strong one. When challenges presented themselves, she'd dealt with them. She'd never had anyone that she could count on to shoulder some of the load. Never had anyone to lean on. Until now.

Instead of telling her to quit being so emotional or

dismissing her concerns by mouthing some meaning-less platitudes, Mitch gave validity to her feelings. The comforting words he murmured meant more to her than he could imagine.

And when he was through talking, he pressed kisses against her hair and across her jaw line. Anna couldn't remember ever feeling so close to him, not even when they were making love. She savored the moment, revel-ing in the closeness, in the feel of his hand against her hair, in his broad chest providing strength and stability.

Being in the arms of the man she loved was truly a piece of heaven on earth.

The man she *loved?*

Anna stiffened as the realization gently slapped her cheeks. Despite her best intentions, she'd fallen back in love with Mitch. But this was different. This wasn't the "he's got a hot body, I love him" passion of her youth. This was a mature emotion. She knew the man, recognized his strengths, understood his weaknesses and still loved him.

She opened her mouth to thank him for his kindness, but her stomach spoke first.

Mitch chuckled.

Anna lifted her head from his chest. "What's so funny?"

"I've never had a woman growl at me before," he said in a teasing tone.

She couldn't help but smile.

He lifted a questioning brow. "Did someone skip dinner?"

"I didn't even think of it," Anna admitted as her

stomach rumbled again, more loudly this time. "I was on the phone with my mom most of the evening."

"You'll feel better once you eat." Mitch brushed her hair back from her face in a gentle gesture then kissed the corner of her mouth. "You relax. I'll scout up something in the kitchen."

Anna couldn't remember the last time she'd felt so pampered. "You're a nice guy, Mitchell Donavan. Anyone ever tell you that?"

His lips eased into a slight smile. "I aim to please."

"You do please me," Anna said. "Very much."

Without warning, he kissed her hard on the lips. "Hold that thought."

Anna's head was still spinning as Mitch left, headed for the kitchen. She wondered what she'd be having for dinner. But even more important, she wondered if he'd be interested in having a woman who was head over heels in love with him for dessert.

Anna was still on the sofa, head back against the cushions, eyes closed, when Mitch returned with the sandwiches.

In all the time they'd spent together, he'd never seen her cry. Her parents' brush with death had clearly shaken her.

He stepped into the room lit only by a Tiffany lamp. There were other lights he could have turned on, but the soft muted glow seemed to fit the mood.

Anna opened her eyes when Mitch placed the tray on the side table next to the sofa. Her eyes were dark and unreadable. "I'm sorry. I'm not usually such a baby."

Mitch dropped down next to her. "It makes me feel good to know you feel safe sharing your feelings with me."

"I trust you," Anna said.

He couldn't imagine a better compliment.

"My mother and I talked about a lot of things today," Anna informed him. "Not just about the accident."

Mitch wasn't sure where she was going with this, but it seemed important to her so he smiled encouragingly.

"Pastor Barbee's sermon got me thinking," Anna said. "I'd always wanted a better relationship with my mom. I decided there was no time like the present to make an overture."

"Why today?" Mitch made a conscious effort to keep his voice even with no hint of judgment.

He must not have been totally successful because Anna's mouth quirked upward.

"Doesn't sound like the best timing, does it?"

Mitch shrugged and remained silent.

"The accident made me realize that life is fragile and I might not get another chance to bridge the gap between us." Anna ignored the sandwiches and took a sip of tea. "I let her know I wanted us to work on having a closer relationship."

Mitch finally understood. "What did she say?"

"She admitted that she may have pushed me too hard when I was a child. But she'd honestly thought I liked being onstage as much as she had at my age. She'd assumed I was as driven as she'd been. That was definitely my fault."

Mitch thought he'd been listening intently, but somewhere his brain must have shut off because suddenly she wasn't making sense. "How is any of it your fault?"

"I didn't make my feelings clear," Anna said. "I must have given off mixed messages. It isn't fair for me to expect someone to read my mind."

Though that didn't make sense to Mitch, it did to Anna and that was what mattered. He took a wedge of sandwich and handed it to her. "Do you feel better about the relationship now?"

"I do." Anna took a bite of the sandwich and chewed. "I just wish I'd taken the initiative earlier. It's so easy to do nothing."

Mitch understood about doing nothing. For years he'd thought about contacting Del. Deep down he hoped that if they could talk one adult to another, he'd finally be able to understand why his dad had left.

He shoved the thought aside. This conversation was about Anna, not about him and his mixed-up family. "So is everything good?"

"Everything is better." The words might be cautious, but the smile on her lips said it all.

Mitch fought back a pang of envy.

"The one take-away I got from this whole thing is that I need to go after what I want." She stared at him from beneath lowered lashes. "Whether it's making peace with my mother or making love with you."

Fire seared his veins. "Making love?"

"I feel so close to you. I need you. I want you." Anna's eyes were hungry and intense. "Stay with me tonight."

Chapter Fifteen

Anna kept any embarrassment from her voice, any hint of uncertainty from her expression. She knew what she wanted. And she wanted Mitch.

Though his gaze smoldered with pent-up passion, he studied her face. "We decided we were going to wait."

"The wait is over," Anna declared.

A smile spread over his lips at her imperious tone. "What about Lauren?"

"Dead to the world." Anna waved a dismissive hand. "A bomb could go off in this house and she wouldn't even roll over."

"All bases should be covered." Mitch paused, then his smile faded and he groaned. "Except the most important one. I don't have a condom."

"Not a problem," Anna said. "When I was in Billings last week picking up some legal stuff for Alex, I stopped by a drugstore and stocked up. You know, just in case one of us got impatient."

Mitch leaned forward and kissed her on the lips. "You are amazing."

"About amazing…I realize that's the goal but it's been a long time for me." Anna gathered her courage and continued the confession. "So I'm not sure 'amazing' will be the word. But it's got to be like riding a bike."

Mitch's lips twitched. "Are you comparing making love to riding a bike?"

"Just thinking aloud." Anna lifted her chin. "Don't worry. It'll come back to me."

Mitch's fingers closed her lips. "Making love is about showing the other person how much you care. Technique doesn't matter."

Anna shot him a doubtful look.

"Let's go to your room." He stood and held out his hand. "I'll show you what I mean."

Anna rose to her feet, not sure why he was being so conventional. "What's wrong with right here?"

"Still the adventurer." The look in Mitch's eyes told her being adventurous was a very good thing. "Only problem is we're not alone."

"Lauren is dead asleep."

"She might surprise us and come to life," Mitch said. "If she decided to come downstairs for something to drink, she might see…well…it's best we go to your room."

Her disappointment must have shown on her face, because Mitch laughed. "I know it's too staid for you, but trust me, I'll make it memorable."

"I have to warn you," Anna said, her gaze never leaving his. "I sleep in a twin bed."

"I have to warn you." Mitch leaned over and trailed a finger down the side of her face. "We're not going to be doing much sleeping."

Anna couldn't recall what happened during the trip up the stairs. There'd been lots of kissing, she remembered that much...mind-numbing kisses that turned her knees to jelly.

Somehow they'd managed to stumble their way to the second-floor landing where Mitch had scooped her up and carried her into her bedroom. He flipped the light switch, turning on the two bedside lamps. They cast a golden glow across the room. The sweet scent of roses from the dish of petals on the dresser contributed to the romantic atmosphere.

"You smell terrific." Mitch leaned close and nuzzled her throat.

"Extra rose petals." Anna arched her neck back, reveling in the sensation of his lips on her skin. And his hands...every time he touched her, everywhere he touched her, seemed new, yet somehow familiar.

"Roses? This time of year?" His tongue circled her ear turning her skin to fire.

"They were brought in for Stacie's wedding," Anna said, when she finally found her voice.

"It's not petals I smell." His fingers found the rubber band holding back her hair and slid it off. "It's the clean, fresh essence of Anna Anderssen. I've never forgotten the scent."

His fingers buried in her hair as his lips scattered kisses everywhere but on her lips. Her breasts tingled and the warmth between her legs turned to an ache. "The clothes have to go."

Even as she spoke, Anna grasped the hem of her tee. But before she could tug it up and over her head, Mitch's hands were on hers, pushing the shirt back down.

"Slow down," he said in a low voice. "We have all night."

Though his voice shook with emotion and there wasn't even a hint of reproach in his words, for a second Anna hesitated. Then she slid her hand under his sweater, feeling his muscles tighten beneath her touch. "The other times we couldn't get naked quick enough."

In fact they'd practically torn the clothes off each other.

"The boy back then couldn't wait." Though his lips quirked upward, his eyes were intense with need. "I've gained some self-control since then."

"It's me, isn't it?" Anna pulled her hand away and took a step back, suddenly realizing how she must look. No wonder he had no problem resisting her. "Give me ten minutes. I'll put on some makeup, do something with this hair and find a sexy little bit of nothing to wear. Really, it won't take—"

"Stop it, Anna," Mitch said firmly, the conviction in his tone stilling her nervous ramblings. "When are you going to realize you're beautiful with or without all those things? You're beautiful just the way you are."

"There isn't a man alive who'd look at me now and say I was beautiful," Anna scoffed.

"*I* think you're beautiful." Mitch cradled her face in his hand, his eyes dark and mesmerizing. "There is no one in this world more beautiful to me than you."

The words had barely left his lips when his arms were around her, pulling her to him, planting kisses across her face.

"I can't believe it," Mitch exclaimed. "We get back together for the sole purpose of finalizing that long-ago breakup and I fall for you all over again."

"Same here," Anna said. "Strange, huh?"

"Not so strange." Mitch ran his hands up and down her back. "I never stopped caring."

"We've been given a second chance." Anna's voice was filled with wonder.

"This time it's going to work," Mitch said. "I can't lose you again, Anna. I won't lose you again."

A flood of emotion as strong as a tidal wave splashed over Anna. They would make this work.

But what's going to happen when he finds out about the baby?

At this moment not even the old fear could diminish her happiness. She'd deal with that worry later. *They'd* deal with that later.

"Tonight will be the celebration of our coming back together." Anna lifted her lips, unable to stay serious. "But instead of the reunion being black-tie, the required attire will be…birthday suit."

Mitch burst out laughing. "You are bound and determined to get me naked."

Anna lifted a brow. "Is that a problem?"

"I was planning on showing you a little finesse this time, instead of getting all wild and crazy."

"I like wild and crazy." Anna shot him a wink, feeling suddenly sassy and beautiful.

The words had barely left her lips when they came together, her hands tearing at his clothes, his hands grabbing at hers.

In less than a minute she was properly attired in her birthday suit. And he looked positively magnificent in his.

She let her gaze linger. Her breath came in short, fast puffs. She'd forgotten just how beautiful Mitch was naked.…

"May I have this dance?" He held out a hand to her.

Anna wondered what he was up to until she became aware of the music in the background. She stifled a groan. When she'd been in her room earlier, she'd turned on the radio. And she'd left it on, tuned to the "all love songs, all the time" station.

She stared at Mitch's outstretched hand. "I don't think I've ever danced naked before."

Mitch smiled. "Always a first time."

"This *is* a reunion celebration." Anna placed her

hand in his and let him pull her close. "And reunions typically involve dancing."

It was Anna's last coherent thought. His body was hot and hard and, as they swayed in time to the love songs, her body responded as if it had awakened starving from a thirteen-year slumber. She was impatient and greedy and determined to partake of everything he had to offer.

Thankfully she'd left her purse in her bedroom, because she doubted Mitch could have made it downstairs to get the condoms.

The coming together was explosive like it had always been...but different, too. There was a gentleness to his caresses, a caring in his kisses and a warmth that mixed with the fire in his eyes and made this reunion extra special.

She needn't have worried about her rusty "skills." Desire, fueled by her feelings for Mitch, drove her responses. Afterward, they cuddled under the blankets, spooned next to each other.

The tension that had gripped her body only hours before had vanished. In its place was a sense of contentment, a feeling that all was right with the world. By the satisfied look in Mitch's eyes, he had no complaints.

"I wish everyone could be as happy as I am right now," Anna murmured, kissing the bend in his arm.

"I think Cassie and Alex are headed in this direction," Mitch said.

Anna knew her boss had sent Cassie flowers after their bowling night. And she'd heard him on the phone to her several times this week.

"I'm happy for Cassie," Anna said. "I'd hoped the failure of her first marriage wouldn't color her feelings for all men."

"As long as Alex doesn't lie to her, he should be okay."

"Lie?"

"I never understood how Jack could lie to Cassie all those years." Mitch's voice was heavy with disappointment. "He should have just leveled with her."

Despite the down comforter and Mitch's warm body, Anna shivered. "Remind me again what he did."

"The night of his bachelor party, he slept with another woman."

Anna had known Jack Dodds since they were children. That behavior didn't sound like the guy she'd known, the one who'd adored Cassie Els since grade school. "That surprises me."

"Their marriage might have been able to survive if he'd told her," Mitch said, "but he never did. Then the woman he'd slept with shows up years later with a kid—his son—in tow. Cassie found out he'd been paying child support all those years."

"Oh my God." Though there wasn't much room in the bed, Anna flipped to face Mitch. "What happened?"

"The truth came out," Mitch said. "He hadn't told her any of this. Not before they were married. Not after."

"She was scared." The words slipped past Anna's lips and it took her a second to realize what she'd said.

"What?"

"I mean, *he* was probably scared," Anna said, her heart racing.

"I guess." Mitch brushed a kiss across her lips. "I don't want to talk about Cassie anymore. Or Alex. Or Jack."

Anna could tell by the flare of heat in his eyes that talking no longer interested him. But she couldn't stop from voicing one final question. "Did Cassie even consider forgiving him?"

"I don't know," Mitch said. "Perhaps if he'd told her early on, but to find out he'd lied to her all those years…I think it was too much for her."

Anna leaned her head against his chest. Right now she stood on the verge of having it all. Or, depending on what she decided to tell Mitch, on the verge of losing it all.

Love was in the air. It was in the melody plucked by the harpist's fingers. It was in the scent of roses that filled the house. Most of all, it was in Stacie's and Josh's eyes when they said their vows in front of a close group of family and friends.

While the backyard had been decorated with an arbor of flowers and a stage had been built for the vows, the unpredictable Montana weather had moved the wedding inside. That was perfectly okay with Anna. She thought the parlor was just as pretty, with candles and flowers everywhere.

Anna saw Mitch standing to the right of Josh. Black tie never looked better. A rush of love rose up inside her. Since their rendezvous Wednesday night, all she'd been able to think about was him.

They hadn't had any time alone since he'd left her bed early Thursday morning. The rehearsal dinner had taken up last night and she hadn't seen him today until they'd walked into the living room together.

"I now pronounce you husband and wife," Pastor Barbee said with unchecked enthusiasm.

Anna brought her focus back to the present just in time to see Stacie kiss her husband.

A lump rose to her throat. She'd been to a gazillion weddings but never had she felt so positive that a couple was going to live happily ever after. The happy ending was what she'd always wanted for her friends. Heck, who she was kidding? *It's what I want for me.*

Music filled the air. Stacie and her new husband walked the short aisle between the wooden chairs where the guests were seated. Lauren and Seth came next, followed by Anna and Mitch.

"You look absolutely delectable," Mitch said in a low growl.

"I was thinking the same about you," Anna teased. "Only I was picturing you naked."

Mitch chuckled. "Great minds obviously think alike."

But the small reception at the house, followed by the dance at the civic center, certainly hadn't afforded any privacy. Like now, she was with Alex while Mitch and Cassie danced.

"I've never had so much fun at a wedding dance." Alex filled a glass with punch and handed it to Anna.

The attorney had loosened his tie and unbuttoned his suit coat. She and Mitch had run into him and Cassie when they were heading for the punch bowl. From the proprietary way Alex's arm had been slung over the pretty brunette's shoulder, it appeared Mitch had been right about that budding romance. That was why Anna wasn't jealous when Cassie had asked Mitch to dance.

As Anna sipped her punch, she glanced around. Based on the number of bodies in the civic center, the streets of Sweet River had to be deserted tonight.

"Nothing brings out the people like a wedding dance." She smiled at the sight of Stacie's brother Tom two-stepping his way across the dance floor. The stiff Midwesterner looked like he was having a good time.

"I'm starting to finally feel a part of this town." There was satisfaction and contentment in Alex's voice.

"That's wonderful." Anna knew how much Alex wanted to be a part of the community. And from what she'd observed, he was on the right track.

"Stacie told me to reach out to people, not just expect to automatically fit in," Alex said. "She was right."

"Your client list has certainly grown," Anna said. "I've seen a marked change just in the few months that I've worked for you."

"The increased revenue is nice," Alex said to Anna, though his attention remained fixed on Cassie, who was returning from the dance floor with Mitch. "But I firmly believe there's more to a happy life than simply having a successful business."

"Yes, there is," Anna said, her heart quickening as Mitch drew close.

"Hey, you." Mitch smiled and slipped an arm around her waist. "Interested in checking out the appetizers? I have it on good authority that the bride made them herself and they're fabulous."

"Hunger calls." Anna wiggled her fingers and smiled her goodbye to Cassie and Alex, now standing arm in arm.

Mitch kept her close as they made their way through the crowd. She couldn't remember the last time she'd felt so happy.

"I wish my parents could have made it back," she said. "Or that I could have gone down there."

"You'll find the time." Mitch gave her arm a squeeze. "I'm just glad you and your mom are back on track."

"Me, too," Anna said. "I can't begin to tell you how good it feels."

"I wish Del and I could have a good talk," Mitch said, his tone turning serious. "I've never really understood why he took off. It's not that I want to be his best friend or anything. I'd just like to understand."

"Find him," Anna urged. "Ask Cassie where she saw him and pay him a visit. What would it hurt?"

"What would what hurt?" Henry asked in a jovial voice, clapping a hand on Mitch's shoulder.

"Henry. Marg." Anna stepped forward. "This is a pleasant surprise. I thought you were at a horse show in Bozeman this weekend."

"Got rescheduled," Henry said. "I didn't care. Gave me the chance to come to the reception and see Mitch dressed like a penguin."

Mitch rolled his eyes and Anna laughed.

"You look lovely," Marg said, her gaze shifting from Mitch to Anna.

"She looks amazing," Mitch agreed. "She's the most beautiful woman in the room."

Anna's cheeks warmed at the compliment.

Henry chuckled. "I think you might be a bit prejudiced."

"Not at all," Mitch said, looking surprisingly serious.

"Now that the horse show is canceled, do you have plans for the weekend?" Anna asked, deliberately changing the subject.

"As a matter of fact we do," Marg said. "Henry and I decided it'd be fun to have some people over to play cards tomorrow night. We'd love to have you and Mitch join us."

Before Anna could say a word, Mitch shook his head. "I'm afraid we can't. Stacie and Josh are opening their gifts—"

Anna tugged on his sleeve. "I forgot to tell you. They changed the gift opening to Sunday afternoon."

"Then I guess we are free." Mitch looked at Anna for confirmation. She nodded.

"Dinner at seven. Cards at eight?" Henry said.

"Works for me." Anna shifted her gaze to Mitch. "You want to pick me up around six-thirty?"

To her surprise, Mitch hesitated. "I'm thinking of going to Billings tomorrow. I'm not sure when I'll get back. How about if I'm not at your house by six-thirty, I'll meet you there?"

"That works." Anna couldn't believe she was actually looking forward to a night of playing pitch.

But she was starting to realize that it wasn't what she was doing, but who she was doing it with, that made the difference.

She leaned back against Mitch and felt his arms close around her. Yes indeed, being with the one you loved made all the difference in the world.

Chapter Sixteen

"I'm sure he's okay." Henry placed a comforting hand on Anna's shoulder as she stared out the window into the darkness.

"He was supposed to be here hours ago." Anna fought to keep her voice steady. "And he's not answering his cell."

She let the lace curtain fall from her cold fingers. Not only had Mitch missed dinner, but it was past ten and the card party had been going on for hours.

Dear God, please keep him safe.

"He'll be okay," Henry said in the hearty voice people used when they wanted you to believe there was nothing to worry about.

"He has to be." Anna blinked back the tears pushing at her lids.

Henry's gaze searched her face. "Sounds like things have gotten serious."

"I love him, Henry," Anna said, her voice thick with emotion. "I can't lose him. Not when we've finally found each other again."

"Come with me." He took her arm and propelled her to the sofa.

The large book-lined study, located at the southern end of Henry's ranch house, was far removed from the conversation and laughter of the card players. It was where Anna had waited for the last hour. She'd eaten dinner. She'd played cards. When she could no longer pretend nothing was wrong, she'd sought refuge in the study.

Anna took a seat and exhaled a shuddering sob. Something was definitely wrong. Mitch would never just not show up. And he certainly wouldn't ignore her calls.

"What went wrong between you and Mitchell all those years ago?" Henry asked. "I never understood what happened."

If any person other than Henry Millstead had broached the question, she'd have immediately shut them down. But she knew he was simply making conversation. Talking was a way to keep his mind and hers off their worries.

"You don't have to tell me if you don't want to," Henry added when the silence lengthened. "It wasn't my place to ask."

"I promised Mitch I'd go with him to the centennial celebration. Instead I dissed him and showed up with Andrew James." Anna didn't care that Mitch thought he was partially to blame. It had been entirely her fault.

"Why did you do that?" Henry's gray brows pulled together. "Didn't you like Mitchell?"

"I wanted to see if I could make him jealous." Anna saw no need to sugarcoat the truth. "I wasn't sure he liked me as much as I liked him."

Henry shook his head. He mumbled something but all she got was "kids." "Sounds like you got your response."

"He was hurt. Angry. But most of all furious that I'd lied to him. I—"

"I still don't like being lied to." Mitch stood in the doorway, his dark hair windblown, his face simmering with rage.

Relief like sweet honey soothed Anna. Only the closed look on his face kept her from flinging herself into his arms.

"I need to know why you chose to lie to me," Mitch demanded.

For one horrific moment Anna thought he was speaking directly to her. Until she realized Mitch's gaze was firmly fixed on Henry.

"Lied to you?" Henry turned to face Mitch head-on. "What are you talking about?"

"I went to see my father today." The muscle in Mitch's jaw tensed. "Or should I say, the man I *thought* was my father."

Marg, who'd followed Mitch to the room, stepped back. "I'll leave you alone so you can discuss this privately."

"No. Stay," Mitch said, keeping his gaze firmly focused on Henry.

Anna started to rise but sank back into the sofa cushions as Mitch stepped forward, his eyes flashing.

"Del had some interesting things to say." Mitch stopped squarely in front of Henry. "For starters he told me I wasn't his son."

Anna gasped.

Mitch's lips turned up in a humorless smile. "Yep, that's right. Apparently my mother was pregnant when she married him. When I was little he thought I was his son. But then he discovered differently."

"Was it because of a blood type?" Henry asked.

"No, it was because Del found out he was sterile." Mitch's gaze pinned Henry. "Why didn't you tell me you were my father?"

Anna couldn't believe her ears. "Henry is your dad?"

Lines of strain edged Henry's mouth. "I wanted to tell you for a long time what I suspected."

"Then why didn't you?" Mitch's hands clenched into fists. "How could you let me live with him? You knew what he was like. Didn't my well-being matter at all to you?"

"Whoa, boy," Henry said. "Give me a chance to explain."

"I wish you would." Mitch's tone was sharp, biting.

"Mitchell." Marg spoke sharply but her eyes were filled with compassion. "Let him speak."

"It's okay, honey," Henry said. "The boy has a right to be upset."

Mitch crossed his arms. "So what's your excuse?"

His jaw was set in a stubborn tilt and his blue eyes were frosty. But Anna could see the hurt behind the belligerent facade and her heart cried for him.

"Your mother and I had a short-lived relationship. My wife had died. Lucy had recently split up with her boyfriend." Henry's eyes took on a faraway glow. "I cared about her. I really did. But after a couple months she told me she was going back to Del. He was the one she loved, the one she'd always loved, not me."

Silence filled the room.

"Then this lovely lady moved to town." Henry gestured to Marg and there was no mistaking his love for her. "And I realized who I was really meant to be with."

Marg moved to his side and took his hand.

"Del was in the military when he and Lucy married. They didn't return to Sweet River until you were five," Henry explained. "I had no reason to think you were my son."

Mitch walked to the window, his back straight as any soldier. "When did you find out?"

"I've never known for sure," Henry said. "When my older brother came to visit me your senior year in high school, he got me thinking. The minute he saw you, he told me you were the spitting image of Grandpa Millstead. That's when I started to wonder."

"You say you didn't suspect anything until I was a senior. What about when I was thirteen? When you gave me a job?" Mitch turned from the window to face Henry. "You expect me to believe you did all that for a stranger?"

"I did it for Lucy's son," Henry said. "Your mother was a special woman. A good friend."

Mitch raked his hands through his hair and began to pace the room, his pain almost palpable.

Anna longed to comfort him but she remained seated. This might be Mitch's only chance to get his questions answered.

"You came to my graduation knowing I was your son." It was a statement, not a question.

"A young man I'd grown to love and respect was graduating," Henry said. "I wanted you to know you had my support. Even if you weren't my son, I'd still have done what I could to ensure you'd succeed."

Anna wasn't sure what Henry was referring to, but from the look on Mitch's face he wasn't so dense.

"You funded the scholarship I was awarded," Mitch said slowly.

"I wanted to give you a chance to get ahead. You were a great kid, Mitch. Whether you were my son or Del's, you deserved the opportunity."

Mitch moved to the sofa and dropped down next to Anna, a stunned look on his face. He rubbed the bridge of his nose with his fingers. "I don't know what to think."

Henry walked over and squeezed Mitch's shoulder. "Give it time. You've got a lot to digest."

"Henry," Marg called softly to her husband. "Why don't you come with me. We'll say goodbye to our guests and give Mitch and Anna some time alone."

Henry hesitated for only a second before following his wife out of the room.

"I'm sorry you had to find out something so important in this way." Anna fumbled for the right words. "I mean, Henry's a great guy. And it's clear he cares."

Mitch jumped to his feet and began pacing. "Why didn't he tell me what he suspected? Even if he didn't know for sure, why did he let me think Del was my dad?"

The face that turned to Anna asked for answers she didn't have to give. She rose to her feet and placed a hand on his arm. "At the time I'm sure it seemed like the right thing to do."

"Lying to someone you care about is *never* the right thing to do," he said between clenched teeth.

Anna took a step back as if she'd been struck.

Mitch didn't seem to notice. He resumed pacing. "I trusted Henry to be honest with me. I never dreamed he'd betray that trust."

Self-preservation told her to keep her mouth shut, but Anna knew these two men cared deeply for each other. She had to do what she could to stop this estrangement from deepening.

"Henry didn't really lie to you," Anna said. "You heard him. He didn't know that you were his son. Not for sure."

"Semantics, Anna," Mitch snapped.

The hand that she'd reached out to him dropped to her side. A sudden chill washed over her. He was right.

A lie of omission made it no less a lie.

"Oh, honey, I'm sorry." Mitch stepped forward, instantly contrite. "There's no reason for me to be so abrupt. I know you're only trying to help."

"All I want is for you to be happy," Anna said, her heart now heavy.

"I just want people not to lie to me," Mitch said. "Is that so much to ask?"

The hardwood beneath Anna's feet was solid and firm. So why did she suddenly feel as if she was sliding down a slippery slope?

"I don't think it's too much to ask." Anna chose her words carefully. "But I think people lie for many reasons, not all of them bad."

"Such as?"

"Such as wanting to protect the person they love," Anna said slowly, her heart pounding against her ribs. "Especially if they know the truth wouldn't change anything and just might hurt that person."

"I understand what you're saying," Mitch said, his gaze thoughtful. "And for most people that might be okay. But not for me."

"Why not?" Anna's voice seemed to come from far away.

Mitch shook his head. "When you grow up with an alcoholic, it's one lie after another. One broken promise after another."

Anna's heart twisted. "That must have been hard."

"I didn't tell you to get sympathy," Mitch said with a slight smile. "I just wanted you to understand why it's so important that we're honest with each other."

His eyes were clear and blue and filled with trust.

Guilt rose inside Anna and with it the realization that she couldn't continue to lie to him. Though her heart ached at the thought of hurting him—he'd already been hurt so much this evening—she had to tell him the truth. "There's something I have to tell you."

He smiled expectantly but when Anna opened her mouth, nothing came out. Perspiration dotted her brow.

"Don't be scared," Mitch said reassuringly. "You can tell me anything."

He wasn't suspicious yet. There was still time to save herself. There was no way he'd find out on his own. Medical records were private. Her secret could stay a secret forever.

She wavered, sorely tempted to take the easy road. But she couldn't do it. A lie of omission was still a lie.

"Remember when I called you all those years ago?" The words tumbled out so fast Anna wondered if he'd even be able to understand what she'd asked.

He slowly nodded.

Anna clasped her hands together to still their trembling. She met his gaze. "I was calling to tell you I was pregnant."

Chapter Seventeen

Once when Del had been drunk he'd shoved Mitch against the wall. The impact had driven all the air from Mitch's lungs. He remembered that feeling. He felt the same way now.

"Pregnant?" The word felt foreign on his tongue.

"When I found out I was scared…so very scared." Anna wrung her hands together. "I didn't know what to do. I called but you were on a date. You'd moved on with your life. I was alone."

He heard the pain in her voice, saw the anguish in her eyes, knew he should tell her he understood. But he didn't understand.

"What happened?" Mitch tried but he couldn't seem

to push the words past his numb lips. He cleared his throat and tried again. "What happened to the baby?"

"I thought I hated it." Her gaze shifted, refusing to meet his eyes. "But I didn't. I know that now. I was just scared and confused."

Unease slid its icy fingers up his spine.

"What happened to the baby?" he repeated.

"I went to Student Health at the college to have the pregnancy confirmed. They gave me the options." Anna drew a shuddering breath. "They also encouraged me to tell the father."

Father. He had a son. Or a daughter. A child he'd never even known existed…

"Where is the child?" His tone demanded rather than asked.

She flinched and her gaze refused to meet his. "There is no child."

"You had an…?"

Tears slipped down her cheeks and for a long moment she didn't respond. Then she squared her shoulders and finally her eyes met his. "My mother and I were barely on speaking terms. You'd made it clear you wanted nothing to do with me. Yes, I made an appointment for an abortion."

Her chin jutted out defiantly but the lost look in her eyes and quivering chin told him she was still haunted by what she'd done.

He wanted to be angry, but her pain wrapped around his heart and became entangled with his until he wasn't sure where hers ended and his began.

"Is that what happened?" He felt tears sting his eyes but he blinked them away. "Did you have an abortion?"

It seemed an obvious conclusion but nothing about this conversation had been normal.

"I miscarried the night before the procedure was scheduled." Anna swiped at her falling tears with the pads of her fingers. "I don't think I'd have kept that appointment. But I'll never know for sure."

Mitch rubbed a hand across his face. He didn't know what to say. Hell, he didn't even know what to think. The only thing he knew was his world had turned upside down. "Anything else?"

"Isn't that enough?" She tried to laugh but it sounded more like a sob. "No, that's all."

In that moment he saw the young girl who'd been so scared and alone, the one who'd felt she had nowhere to turn. And the one person she'd called—*him*—had let her down.

He wanted to say something reassuring, but the words wouldn't come. It was as if the circuits leading from his brain to his mouth had shut down.

As the seconds ticked by, the tiny sliver of hope in Anna's eyes faded, replaced by a stark emptiness. She leaned over and grabbed her bag.

"If it makes you feel better, you can't hate me any more than I hate myself," she said so softly he wasn't sure if he'd imagined the words. Then, before he could even blink, she slipped from the room and the door clicked shut behind her.

Mitch told himself to go after her but instead he

moved to the window. He watched her walk with slumped shoulders to her vehicle. Watched the Jeep head down the drive toward the road. Watched the taillights disappear from view.

He wasn't sure how long he stood there, staring out into the darkness, watching as one by one the other guests left. When the last car pulled out of the yard, Mitch heard the door open.

"Everyone is gone," Henry said. "I need to check on the roan. Care to join me?"

One of the wild horses Mitch had "adopted" had stepped in a gopher hole and injured her leg. Henry had been keeping her in a stall while it healed.

It was understandable that Henry would ask him to check on the filly. After all, she was Mitch's horse. But the request went beyond that and they both knew it.

"I'd like to see how she's doing." Mitch turned around. "I want you to know I appreciate everything you've done for me. You didn't need to do any of it."

Henry's tense expression eased into a smile. In many ways he'd been a victim of Del's lies, too. Del could have revealed the truth many years ago. "Like I said, I wanted to help you out. After all, we're family."

Mitch nodded. "That we are."

With those three little words, the remaining tension between them disappeared. Mitch realized in the span of minutes that he'd gone from having an absentee dad to having a stepmother, two older sisters and a father who'd been there for him since he was thirteen.

On their way out of the house, they passed Marg.

The lines of worry between her brows eased at Henry's wink.

Mitch tried not to think of Anna, but even the brisk north wind couldn't drive her from his thoughts. He couldn't forget the pain in her eyes, and he couldn't forget the baby.

Given different circumstances, he could be the father of a boy as active and headstrong as Cassie's Trenton. Or a girl as bright and creative as Seth's Dani. But that wasn't how it had played out. And despite his own regret for what might have been, he realized the difficult situation Anna had faced alone. All because he'd been a jerk on the phone.

Henry pulled open the large door leading to the stable. "I saw Anna leave. Looked to me like she'd been crying."

"Didn't have anything to do with what was going on between you and me," Mitch said in answer to the unspoken question.

"I suppose that's something." Henry moved to the stall holding the roan. Lifting the latch, he stepped inside and Mitch followed. Seconds later, after checking the bandage, they stepped out of the stall.

"She's going to be fine," Henry said in satisfaction.

"She's got a lot of spunk."

"Anna's got spunk, too," Henry said. "But when she left, she looked beaten."

"There was an incident in the past," Mitch said, keeping the explanation deliberately vague. "We talked about it."

"You talked about it." Henry put a boot on the gate. "But you didn't put it to bed."

The roan met Mitch's gaze. Just like before, something in her eyes reminded him of Anna. "Put what to bed?"

"My mother used to always say that before you put yourself to bed, you need to put any troubles to bed. Deal with issues, make amends, kiss and make up."

"I'm not sure that's possible." Mitch kept his gaze fixed on the filly.

"Do you love Anna?"

Mitch scowled. "What kind of question is that?"

"Do you love her?" Henry repeated.

"Yes," Mitch admitted to the roan. "Very much."

"And she loves you."

Mitch watched the roan move to the gate. He scratched the tiny patch of white between her eyes. "I'm not sure about that."

"I am," Henry said. "She told me so."

"When?"

"While we were waiting and worrying about you." Henry's brows pulled together. "Why didn't you call and let us know you were running late? Anna must have rung your cell five or six times. Why didn't you call her back?"

"I was so thrown by what Del had told me that I turned off my phone. I needed time to think."

"Time to think is good," Henry said. "But never at the expense of worrying those who love you."

There was no mistaking the loving censure, the sort

he'd always gotten from Henry. But Mitch realized it was no more than he deserved. He'd thought only of himself. Just like he had all those years ago. Back then there had been nothing stopping him from calling her back. Nothing but his own stubborn pride.

"Now about this matter that the two of you discussed." Henry paused. "Is it something you can live with? Something you can get past?"

Was it only Mitch's imagination or did the roan prick up her ears?

Mitch thought of Anna, the girl he'd once loved. The woman he now loved. "Yes," he said. "This is something we can definitely get past."

"Then go to her, son." Henry looked pleased to use the word. It felt right to Mitch, too.

"Put to bed the matter that is keeping you apart," Henry urged.

Still Mitch hesitated. After how he'd acted, how could he expect Anna to forgive him? What would he say to her?

"The words will come," Henry said as if he'd read Mitch's mind. "Let your love do the talking and it will all work out."

The roan tossed her head and whinnied.

Mitch only hoped they were right. Because his future happiness was at stake.

By the time Anna pulled into her driveway, the tears had stopped but her hands still shook. On the way home she'd had to fight the urge to bypass Sweet River and just keep driving.

Only the thought of how upsetting her absence would be to Stacie kept Anna from giving in to the impulse. Opening the gifts tomorrow at the house was as much a part of the wedding as the ceremony itself. Anna refused to ruin her friend's festivities.

She rested her head against the steering wheel, utterly drained. She'd known it was foolish telling Mitch about the baby when he was so upset. Yet she hadn't been able to bring herself to lie to him anymore.

At least he hadn't screamed at her, like she'd envisioned. But his hurt look had sliced her heart into pieces. The silence had been worse than words because she'd been forced to imagine what he was thinking, what he was holding back.

Of course she hadn't expected it to go well. Hoped, yes. Prayed, absolutely. But in her heart she'd known that to expect him to forgive her was expecting more than she deserved.

"Anna."

A knock on the car window roused her from her stupor. She turned to find Lauren's worried face staring at her through the glass.

"I'm okay." Anna lifted her head and did her best to force a reassuring smile. "Just tired."

Lauren stepped back as Anna grabbed her keys and bag and pushed open the door.

Despite the restraint her friend had shown, Anna expected the questions to start the minute she got out of the car. Instead, Lauren clucked like a mother hen and slipped her arm through Anna's, helping her friend negotiate what seemed to be an impossible distance from the car to the house.

Though the wind had stopped blowing and the air brushing Anna's face came from the south, she shivered. Cold gripped her soul. She couldn't imagine ever feeling warm again.

"I'd just made a pot of tea," Lauren said, when they stepped inside.

Anna opened her mouth to say she was too tired, too sad, too…something…but Lauren had already hurried off, calling over her shoulder for Anna to have a seat in the parlor.

There was nothing stopping Anna from heading upstairs. It wasn't as if Lauren would come to her room and drag her out. Yet Anna hesitated. Her room would be quiet and she wasn't sure she wanted to be alone with her thoughts. So, instead of trudging up the stairs to certain solitude, she made a right and took a seat on the sofa.

She slung her purse on the cushion next to her and the contents tumbled out. Mascara. Powder. Lip gloss. Anna eyed the products for a long second. From the sounds coming from the kitchen, it appeared she had time to do some touch-up. Scooping up the items, she dumped them back into the bag.

What did it matter what she looked like? What did it matter that her eyes were puffy and her lipstick chewed off? All that mattered was the truth had come out and the fallout had been the loss of the only man she would ever love.

"I'm sorry I took so long." Lauren bustled into the room, carrying a tray of tea and chocolates. "I know we said we were going to try to stay away from the sweets…but this seemed like a good night to splurge."

"I must really look bad." Anna sighed and poured tea from the porcelain pot into her cup.

"I wouldn't say *bad*." Lauren popped a chocolate into her mouth. "But you do look sad."

Anna sniffed. "I am sad."

She shouldn't have said the words. Anna realized it the moment they left her lips. Simply voicing her feelings was enough to bring tears flooding back.

"I'm sorry." Anna's voice wobbled. "I'm not good company. I should go to my room."

She started to rise but Lauren's hand manacled her wrist. "Do you really want to be alone right now?"

Anna quit tugging at Lauren's hand and sat down. She slowly shook her head.

"If you want to talk about what's troubling you, that's fine. If you want to listen to me ramble about my babysitting adventures with your niece, that's okay, too. Or if you want to sit in silence, I'll zip my mouth."

Anna appreciated Lauren's restraint and the choices. "Tell me about your night with Dani."

Seth had called shortly before Anna had left for the Millstead ranch, needing a last-minute sitter. She'd heard the relief in his voice when Lauren had volunteered.

"We played dolls and took turns doing each other's hair." Despite the late hour, Lauren's eyes sparkled. "Dani is a great kid."

"Her dad isn't so bad, either," Anna said, wiping the last of her tears away.

"Your brother?" Lauren's cheeks pinked. "He's okay, I guess."

"Okay?" Anna lifted a brow. "I've seen the way you look at him. You think he's hot. Don't even bother trying to say differently."

"Okay, he is handsome," Lauren admitted. "And he's got a great body."

"Now the truth comes out," Anna crowed.

"But your Mitch is just as good-looking," Lauren said diplomatically.

The icy band tightened around Anna's heart.

"He's not 'my' Mitch." Anna shifted her gaze to the tray and took her time adding two lumps of sugar to her tea. "We broke up tonight. This time for good. After what I told him, he'll never want to talk to me again. And I don't blame him."

Anna clamped her mouth shut. What was she doing? Encouraging Lauren to ask more questions so she'd be forced to tell her friend the whole sordid story?

"What did you tell him?" Lauren asked, almost on cue.

The psychologist had never been one to pussyfoot around. If she had a question, she asked it. However, she always respected a person's right to refuse to answer.

But Anna wasn't going to take a "get out of jail free" pass this time. This was a night for honesty. To hell with the consequences.

"I told him I'd once been pregnant with his baby." Anna sat back and waited for the explosion.

She waited.

And waited.

And waited.

After a long minute ticked by, Lauren took a sip of tea. "Go on."

"Is that all you're going to say?" Anna jumped to her feet, nearly upsetting the tray. "I tell you I was once pregnant. A pregnancy you knew nothing about and all you can say is 'go on'?"

By the end of her diatribe, Anna was practically shouting. Lauren didn't flinch.

"This is serious stuff," Lauren said, her eyes filled with understanding. "Something that you need to tell me in your own way and time. I'm your friend, Anna. I love you and I hope you know I'm here for you."

Lauren's kind words punctured Anna's anger and left her drained. She took a deep breath, clasped her hands together and dropped back to the sofa. "Mitch and I started dating the summer after my senior year in high school."

This time the story came easier. Lauren occasionally asked for clarification but most of all, she just listened. By the time Anna finished the story, ending with her walking out of Henry's house…alone…Lauren's eyes were filled with compassion.

"You're a strong woman, Anna Anderssen," Lauren said. "Not many eighteen-year-olds could have gone through all that and come out intact."

"I'm not intact." Anna felt tears push at her lids. "I'm a mess."

"You returned to your hometown, made amends with the man you had childishly treated all those years ago and even had the courage to fall in love with him again." Admiration underscored Lauren's words. "That doesn't sound like someone who's a mess."

"Mitch can't forgive me." Though it was nothing more than she expected, disappointment still enveloped Anna.

"It's hard to know if he does or not," Lauren said. "But before we focus on Mitch, I'd like to know if you've forgiven yourself?"

Unease slithered up Anna's spine. She eyed the door, wondering if it would be rude to call it a night.

Before she could make a move, Lauren leaned forward and took Anna's hands in hers. "When are you going to forgive yourself?" Lauren said softly. "You were a child. You did the best you could."

"I didn't." The guilt welled up from deep inside Anna. "I could have called Mitch back. I could have tried harder to—"

"None of this would be an issue if I'd called you back."

Anna's breath caught in her throat at the sound of the familiar baritone. She jumped to her feet and whirled.

"I rang the bell," Mitch said from his position in the doorway. "No one answered. The door was unlocked so I came in."

"This is a private conversation." Lauren's brows pulled together, her tone sharp. "How long have you been standing there?"

"Long enough to know Anna and I've got some talkin' to do." His gaze met Anna's. "I'd like to do it now, if that's okay with you."

Chapter Eighteen

Anna had never expected to see Mitch again. Yet, here he was, his expression watchful and surprisingly calm.

"Do you feel up to talking to Mitch?" The determined glint in Lauren's eyes told Anna if the answer was no, she'd personally show him the door.

"Mitch is right. We need to talk." Though her voice sounded like it came from far away, at least it was steady and strong. While she'd made her share of mistakes, Anna was determined to face the rest of her life with her head held high.

"If you're sure…" Lauren's gaze shifted from Anna to Mitch, before returning to Anna.

"I'm positive." Anna added a decisive nod for Lauren's benefit.

"I'll leave you two alone." When Lauren rose and turned to go, Anna grasped her hand.

"Thank you for being such a good friend." Though she felt stronger than she had all night, Anna held tight to Lauren's hand as if it were a life preserver and she was about to go under.

Lauren smiled understandingly. She gently pried Anna's fingers from hers. "I'll be upstairs in my room if you need me."

Anna watched her friend leave the parlor. She waited until she heard Lauren's footfalls on the stairs before she turned her attention to Mitch. "I didn't expect to see you again."

A look of pain crossed his face. "I acted like a jerk tonight and I'm sorry."

Though she could hear the furnace cranking out the heat, Anna wrapped her arms around herself to stave off the cold. "It's me who is sorry."

"It was all my fault." Mitch's jaw jutted out. "When we slipped into that closet, I had a good idea what was going to happen. I knew I didn't have a condom but I went anyway."

"It's always been hard for me to think rationally when you were around," Anna said.

"Same here," Mitch said, his lips widening in that heart-stopping grin she loved so much. A grin she was going to miss.

"Why are you here?" Anna didn't mean to be rude but talking like this, as if things between them were normal and not irrevocably broken, was killing her. "I thought we said everything there was to say at the ranch."

"*You* did." Mitch took a step forward and the spicy scent of his cologne enveloped her. "I'm the one who left so much unsaid."

Anna tensed her shoulders and prepared herself for the mental blows. "Go ahead. Say what you came to say."

"I've got so much to apologize for that it's difficult to know where to begin." His blue eyes shimmered with emotion. "When we started dating, I deliberately kept my feelings to myself. I was terrified of being open with you. If I had let you know how special you were to me, you wouldn't have needed to come up with a scheme to make me jealous. You'd have known how much I cared."

"I wasn't good at sharing my feelings, either," Anna admitted. "Otherwise you'd have known that Andrew meant nothing to me. You were the one I wanted, the one I always wanted, not him."

"And to not call you back, that was inexcusable." His voice, though well-controlled, shook with emotion. "When I think how scared you must have been… There aren't enough words to let you know how sorry I am. If I could go back in time and change my behavior, I'd do it in a heartbeat."

"You were a boy." Anna rested a hand on his arm.

"What's my excuse now?" Mitch asked with a self-deprecating laugh.

The fire crackled behind her but Anna paid it no mind. "I don't understand…."

"When we started dating again, I gave you my word that I'd always be there for you."

"You kept that promise," Anna said.

"No. No. No. I haven't." Mitch paced a few steps, raked a hand through his hair then turned to face Anna. "You tried calling me earlier. I didn't answer. I was so caught up in what *I* was feeling that I never once stopped to consider *your* feelings. I never even considered how worried you must have been."

Anna didn't know what to say. He was right. Her stomach had been twisted in knots until he'd walked through the door.

"Once again, I wasn't there for you." The self-loathing in his eyes took her by surprise. Was that why he was here? To seek some sort of absolution?

"I forgive you, Mitch." Anna hoped he heard the sincerity in her voice. The last thing she wanted was to leave him burdened with his own guilt. And even if she hadn't already forgiven him, the bald hope in his expression would have been impossible to resist.

"So things are back to the way they were?" Mitch asked.

"Between us?"

"Of course between us."

They'd talked about his culpability and his regret…but not about the elephant in the room. The one thing ensuring that nothing could ever be the same between them again. "Have you forgotten I considered aborting your baby?"

"Those were difficult times," Mitch said softly.

"There is no way of knowing what you would have done. You were being forced to make decisions no eighteen-year-old should have to make alone. It would all have been different if I'd been there for you."

For so many years, Anna had carried a heavy weight of guilt like a tightly woven shawl around her shoulders. With his words, it began to slip and she felt something lost and aching in her heart begin to heal. "You don't hate me?"

The look on his face would have been comical in any other situation. "I could never hate you."

"Do you forgive me?"

"There's nothing to forgive." His look told her that he spoke the truth. "So is everything okay with us?" Mitch repeated.

The shawl dropped to the floor and pooled at her feet. She kicked it aside as her heart began to sing. "Very much okay."

He grabbed her hand and tugged her to him, wrapping her in his arms and holding her like he'd never let her go. "Henry told me that when you love someone you should strive to put any troubles between you to bed."

"Sounds like good advice." After a second Anna lifted her head, her heart thudding against her ribs. "Did you say...*love?*"

Mitch brushed a strand of hair back from her face and stared into her blue eyes. A feeling of rightness washed over him and the words he'd been longing to say spilled from his heart. "I love you, Anna."

"Truly?" Her voice rose and broke.

"Madly. Deeply. Completely."

The words had barely left his lips when Mitch found himself with his arms full of a sobbing, laughing Anna.

"I love you truly, madly, deeply, completely, too," she said once she could talk again.

He pulled her closer, feeling for the first time that everything was going to be all right. He nuzzled her hair. "Putting problems to bed has never felt so good."

"I know something that will feel even better," Anna said, pressing kisses along his jaw. "Putting *me* to bed."

His body tightened as he covered her mouth with his. They kissed until they were both breathless and dizzy. His heart was still beating a thousand beats a minute when she pulled away and headed for the stairs. "Last one with their clothes on is a rotten egg."

"Anything to get me naked," Mitch said with a laugh, then took off running.

Epilogue

Anna gazed over the frozen waters of the penny pond. "If we're going ice fishing, why did we leave the gear in the car?"

Mitch took her hand, threading his fingers through hers before leaning over to press his lips against hers. The world tilted sideways and the world of ice augers and fishing poles was forgotten.

When the kiss ended, Anna rested her head against his chest and embraced the beautiful sunset. When he'd stopped by Sew-fisticated, the eclectic shop in The Hattan housing everything from yarns and quilting supplies to a seamstress corner featuring Anna's designs, she and Cassie had been getting ready for their grand opening next week.

Going fishing so late in the day made little sense, but Mitch had been on a business trip for the past two days and she was eager to spend time with him.

The past month had spoiled her. Anytime they weren't working, they were together. They'd gone bowling with Alex and Cassie, to the movies with Josh and Stacie and even had lasagna at the Barbees'. And then there were the Sunday dinners they'd spent with Henry and Marg. It had been a blessing to see the relationship continue to build between Mitch and his new family.

"What's making you smile?" Mitch tightened his hold, his breath tickling her ear.

"I never knew I could be this happy." Anna drew back far enough to look into his eyes. "I have wonderful friends. A new business. And a man I love more than anything. I have everything I could ever want."

"I can think of one thing you're missing."

"What would that be?"

"A husband."

Anna's mouth went dry. Her heart tripped over itself when Mitch reached into his pocket, pulled out a tiny velvet box and dropped down to one knee.

"Years ago, I threw a penny into this pond and made a wish. I wished that you and I would be together forever." His voice turned husky. "Today I'm asking if you'll help me make that wish come true. I love you, Anna. More than life itself. I'd be the happiest man on this earth if you'd agree to be my wife."

He flipped open the box and the large sparkly

diamond caught and scattered the rays of the setting sun. "Will you marry me, Anna?"

Anna gazed at the face of the man she'd known since she'd been a girl. They were older and wiser now. Through struggles and disappointments, they'd grown into the people they were meant to be. She couldn't imagine loving anyone more.

"Anna?"

The endearing sense of uncertainty in his voice tugged at her heartstrings.

"I would be honored to be your wife," Anna said and when he slid the ring on her finger, her heart overflowed.

He rose to his feet and held her at arm's length. "We are going to be so happy."

"Ecstatically happy," Anna agreed. Under the glorious Montana sky, she'd found what she'd been searching for all these years. And it had been here waiting for her—the peace that comes with forgiveness, the warmth that comes from a community of family and friends, and most of all, the bliss that comes from finding your one true love.

When Mitch pulled her to him and spun her around, Anna laughed with sheer joy knowing she was finally home.

* * * * *

Celebrate 60 years of pure reading pleasure with Harlequin!

To commemorate the event, Harlequin Intrigue®
is thrilled to invite you to the wedding of
The Colby Agency's J. T. Baxley and his bride,
Eve Mattson.

That is, of course, if J.T. can find the woman
who left him at the altar. Considering he's a
private investigator for one of the top agencies
in the country—the best of the best—that
shouldn't be a problem. The real setback is that
his bride isn't who she appears to be…and her
mysterious past has put them both in danger.

*Enjoy an exclusive glimpse of Debra Webb's
latest addition to*
THE COLBY AGENCY:
ELITE RECONNAISSANCE DIVISION

THE BRIDE'S SECRETS

Available August 2009 from Harlequin Intrigue®.

The dark figures on the dock were still firing. The bullets cutting through the surface of the water without the warning boom of shots told Eve they were using silencers.

That was to her benefit. Silencers decreased the accuracy of every shot and lessened the range.

She grabbed for the rocks. Scrambled through the darkness. Bumped her knee on a boulder. Cursed.

Burrowing into the waist-deep grass, she kept low and crawled forward. Faster. Pushed harder. Needed as much distance as possible.

Shots pinged on the rocks.

J.T. scrambled alongside her.

He was breathing hard.

They had to stay close to the ground until they reached the next row of warehouses. Even though she was relatively certain they were out of range at this point, she wasn't taking any risks. And she wasn't slowing down.

J.T. had to keep up.

The splat of a bullet hitting the ground next to Eve had her rolling left. Maybe they weren't completely out of range.

She bumped J.T. He grunted.

His injured arm. Dammit. She could apologize later.

Half a dozen more yards.

Almost in the clear.

As she reached the cover of the alley between the first two warehouses she tensed.

Silence.

No pings or splats.

She glanced back at the dock. Deserted.

Time to run.

Her car was parked another block down.

Pushing to her feet, she sprinted forward. The wet bag dragged at her shoulder. She ignored it.

By the time she reached the lot where her car was parked, she had dug the keys from her pocket and hit the fob. Six seconds later she was behind the wheel. She hit the ignition as J.T. collapsed into the passenger seat. Tires squealed as she spun out of the slot.

"What the hell did you do to me?"

From the corner of her eye she watched him shake his head in an attempt to clear it.

He would be pissed when she told him about the tranquilizer.

She'd needed him cooperative until she formulated a plan. A drug-induced state of unconsciousness had been the fastest and most efficient method to ensure his continued solidarity.

"I can't really talk right now." Eve weaved into the right lane as the street widened to four lanes. What she needed was traffic. It was Saturday night—shouldn't be that difficult to find as soon as they were out of the old warehouse district.

A glance in the rearview mirror warned that their unwanted company had caught up.

Sensing her tension, J.T. turned to peer over his left shoulder.

"I hope you have a plan B."

She shot him a look. "There's always plan G." Then she pulled the Glock out of her waistband.

Cutting the steering wheel left, she slid between two vehicles. Another veer to the right and she'd put several cars between hers and the enemy.

She was betting they wouldn't pull out the firepower in the open like this, but a girl could never be too sure when it came to an unknown enemy.

Deep blending was the way to go.

Two traffic lights ahead the marquee of a movie theater provided exactly the opportunity she was looking for.

The digital numbers on the dash indicated it was just past midnight. Perfect timing. The late movie would be purging its audience into the crowd of teenagers who liked hanging out in the parking lot.

She took a hard right onto the property that sported a twelve-screen theater, numerous fast-food hot spots and a chain superstore. Speeding across the lot, she selected a lane of parking slots. Pulling in as close to the theater entrance as possible, she shut off the engine and reached for her door.

"Let's go."

Thankfully he didn't argue.

Rounding the hood of her car, she shoved the Glock into her bag, then wrapped her arm around J.T.'s and merged into the crowd.

With her free hand she finger-combed her long hair. It was soaked, as were her clothes. The kids she bumped into noticed, gave her death-ray glares.

They just didn't know.

As she and J.T. moved in closer to the building, she grabbed a baseball cap from an innocent bystander. The crowd made it easy. The kid who owned the cap had made it even easier by stuffing the cap bill-first into his waistband at the small of his back.

Pushing through the loitering crowd, she made her way to the side of the building next to the main entrance. She pushed J.T. against the wall and dropped her bag to the ground. Peeled off her tee and let it fall.

His gaze instantly zeroed in on her breasts, where the cami she wore had glued to her skin like an extra layer. A zing of desire shot through her veins.

Not the time.

With a flick of her wrist she twisted her hair up and clamped the cap atop the blonde mass.

"They're coming," J.T. muttered as he gazed at some point beyond her.

"Yeah, I know." She planted her palms against the wall on either side of him and leaned in. "Keep your eyes open. Let me know when they're inside."

Then she planted her lips on his.

* * * * *

Will J.T. and Eve be caught in the moment?
Or will Eve get the chance to reveal all of her
secrets?
Find out in
THE BRIDE'S SECRETS
by Debra Webb
Available August 2009 from Harlequin Intrigue®.

We'll be spotlighting a different series every month throughout 2009 to celebrate our 60th anniversary.

LOOK FOR
HARLEQUIN INTRIGUE®
IN AUGUST!

To commemorate the event, Harlequin Intrigue® is thrilled to invite you to the wedding of the Colby Agency's J.T. Baxley and his bride, Eve Mattson.

Look for *Colby Agency: Elite Reconnaissance*

THE BRIDE'S SECRETS
BY DEBRA WEBB

Available August 2009

www.eHarlequin.com

Harlequin® Historical
Historical Romantic Adventure!

From *USA TODAY* bestselling author

Margaret Moore

THE VISCOUNT'S KISS

When Lord Bromwell meets a young woman on the mail coach to Bath, he has no idea she is Lady Eleanor Springford—until *after* they have shared a soul-searing kiss!

The nature-mad viscount isn't known for his spontaneous outbursts of romance—and the situation isn't helped by the fact that the woman he is falling for is fleeing a forced marriage....

The Viscount and the Runaway...

Available August 2009
wherever you buy books.

HH29557

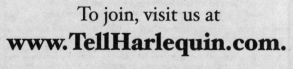

REQUEST YOUR FREE BOOKS!

2 FREE NOVELS PLUS 2 FREE GIFTS!

SPECIAL EDITION®

Life, Love and Family!

YES! Please send me 2 FREE Silhouette Special Edition® novels and my 2 FREE gifts (gifts are worth about $10). After receiving them, if I don't wish to receive any more books, I can return the shipping statement marked "cancel." If I don't cancel, I will receive 6 brand-new novels every month and be billed just $4.24 per book in the U.S. or $4.99 per book in Canada. That's a savings of at least 15% off the cover price! It's quite a bargain! Shipping and handling is just 50¢ per book.* I understand that accepting the 2 free books and gifts places me under no obligation to buy anything. I can always return a shipment and cancel at any time. Even if I never buy another book from Silhouette, the two free books and gifts are mine to keep forever.

235 SDN EYN4   335 SDN EYPG

Name	(PLEASE PRINT)	
Address		Apt. #
City	State/Prov.	Zip/Postal Code

Signature (if under 18, a parent or guardian must sign)

Mail to the **Silhouette Reader Service:**
IN U.S.A.: P.O. Box 1867, Buffalo, NY 14240-1867
IN CANADA: P.O. Box 609, Fort Erie, Ontario L2A 5X3

Not valid to current subscribers of Silhouette Special Edition books.

Want to try two free books from another line?
Call 1-800-873-8635 or visit www.morefreebooks.com.

* Terms and prices subject to change without notice. Prices do not include applicable taxes. Sales tax applicable in N.Y. Canadian residents will be charged applicable provincial taxes and GST. Offer not valid in Quebec. This offer is limited to one order per household. All orders subject to approval. Credit or debit balances in a customer's account(s) may be offset by any other outstanding balance owed by or to the customer. Please allow 4 to 6 weeks for delivery. Offer available while quantities last.

Your Privacy: Silhouette is committed to protecting your privacy. Our Privacy Policy is available online at www.eHarlequin.com or upon request from the Reader Service. From time to time we make our lists of customers available to reputable third parties who may have a product or service of interest to you. If you would prefer we not share your name and address, please check here. ☐